TERRY HOPKINS

THE EZRA GATEWAY

This edition first published in paperback by
Michael Terence Publishing in 2023
www.mtp.agency

ISBN 9781800944671

Michael Terence
Publishing

For Pin…

Fire was discovered and used by early humans over a million years ago to heat, cook and survive.

Over the years, as time moved forward man used fire for light, some as a weapon.

Fire has caused great historical moments, 48BC the burning of the Great Library of Alexandria, 1666 The Great Fire of London, 1835 The Great Fire of New York.

Even in modern times, fires like Bradford and Kings Cross released this uncontrollable animal resulting in great loss and pain.

There are some who utilise its power to commit or cover their crimes and firefighters from across the world stand in its way to do battle, and the investigators to search for the truth.

1

47 seconds after the digital display on the clock flipped to 03:38, a gentle vibration began, followed by a low chirping tone just loud enough for the human brain to pick up and interpret. The small black pager lay on the bedside cabinet and barely moved in the 10 seconds of vibration, but the low chirping sound continued until Robert 'Bob' Kennedy rolled over and with his eyes still closed, in a well-practised drill, moved swiftly to silence the noise before the interruption woke his wife. For 32 years Sally Kennedy had become used to Bob's unexpected callouts so even at this quiet time of the morning she never murmured or stirred.

Slowly and silently, he slipped out of bed and put on a black silk kimono dressing gown, not his normal sort of thing but as a present from his daughter the previous Christmas, he had grown to enjoy wearing it in the summer months. Stealthily, he headed downstairs to the kitchen and before looking at the pager message, he flicked the kettle on and sat at the breakfast bar. Giving a slight yawn and stretch, he checked the message for an explanation for this rude awakening on a Sunday morning. As normal the information was short and to the point 'FCC URGENT ASAP' a message he had received hundreds of times over the last 12 years in the Fire Safety Enforcement and Investigation Team. The last five of those years had followed his promotion to Senior Fire Investigation Officer for the London Fire Brigade, affectionately known as the LFB.

While the kettle began to heat up, Bob picked up the phone in the kitchen and dialled the number for Fire Control without thinking, a number permanently ingrained in his memory. Within one ring the call was answered.

"Morning Bob, sorry for the intrusion but we have a fatal property fire that needs your attendance."

"Morning Carol, it's ok I wasn't really asleep anyway," he lied.

"What time do you need me?"

The normal protocol was to attend with an assembled team and a Scene Of Crime Officer or SOCO, generally at the start of daytime, between around 8 or 9 o'clock. This allowed daylight to be used without requiring floodlights for either the whole scene or some external areas for longer periods of time in the initial investigation.

"Sorry, Sir," Carol's voice suddenly turned formal, "the request has been made for you to attend as soon as you can."

There was a split-second pause before he replied,

"Unusual, Carol; is it a high-profile incident or request from above?"

"No, the incident commander on scene specifically asked for you and as soon as possible."

Again, Bob paused.

"Has the Fire Investigation Team not responded?"

"Yes," she replied, "the FIT team have been and gone."

Although Bob's next pause was slightly longer, just as he was going to ask his next question Carol pre-empted his thoughts, "We questioned the Incident Commander over normal service procedures, but he has stated that he won't leave the fireground until you have attended."

As the information sank in that could result in a disciplinary for an officer not following normal service procedures, Bob asked,

"Who is the incident commander?"

He was expecting an unfamiliar name or a newly-promoted junior officer, certainly not the one he was given.

"Watch Commander Bryers sir, South Richmond, Red Watch."

Carol gave the information in a formal tone, just in case

things ended up in further action or logged in any reports. But that was never going to happen.

"What's the address, Carol?"

Bob made a quick note on the kitchen shopping list board.

"Carol, inform Watch Commander Bryers I will be there within the hour."

He flicked the kettle back on and quietly headed back upstairs to dress. Kissing his wife on the head, he turned and as he left the room Sally murmured, "Be careful."

As the kettle boiled for the third time, he pushed his normal prepared morning cup to one side and took a silver metal travel mug out of the cupboard, quickly filled it with a single spoonful of sugar, a tea bag, a splash of milk then topped with hot water. Leaving by the side door, he walked to his brigade car, a two-year-old Land Rover Discovery of high spec. Not the normal officer's car, but he always maintained the need to respond, whatever the weather or outside conditions could throw at him and therefore the normal Ford Focus Estate was totally impractical.

Placing the travel mug in the cup holder and starting the car, he entered the incident address into the sat nav and slowly pulled out of his drive onto the road, heading south towards Richmond Bridge.

2

The drive to 87 Oaklands Close was a short run of about 35 minutes at that time in the morning without the usual rush hour or daily traffic which could have easily added another hour to the trip. Bob's mind drifted back to his memories of attending the Fire Brigade Training Centre many years before where, as firefighter recruits, he and Steve Bryers had formed a close relationship through the three and a half months of basic training before both being stationed together at Abbot Road Fire Station, near the East India Docks. Although placed on different watches, Bob on Green and Steve on Red, they always spent their social time together, initially cycling or watching Leyton Orient's home games before in later years taking up golf and playing whenever time allowed at Sundridge Golf Club.

After the early years of their careers, their paths began to take different directions with Bob rising up the promotion ladder quickly as his thirst for knowledge was greater than Steve's who always preferred the hands-on side of the job. Steve was an exceptionally gifted officer on the fireground with no incident ever fazing or making him feel as if he couldn't deal with it, he would always stand up to whatever was thrown his way. Apart from golf, their families would ritually gather for events, birthdays, anniversaries and Christmas dinner was always shared, although this could often be a day or two later depending on shifts. During these social moments, work was strictly off-line unless it was to recite a funny memory or job over a glass of port. They did from time to time meet professionally on jobs requiring investigation but apart from the information required it was a quick, "Hi mate, how's things?" and normally followed with, "see you Saturday for golf."

What became unsettling for Bob as he drove on was why had Steve broken from normal procedures which he knew could put him in hot water. He knew he could think of a reasonable explanation to help his friend but the whole process could be awkward and there were only so many favours you could ask of your senior officers; it didn't change the fact he was taking a big risk. But why the urgency unless for someone or something highly sensitive, maybe even personal?

As he headed across Richmond Bridge, dawn was beginning to break and the first distant rays of sun began to punch through the light cloud. It's going to be a nice warm day he thought, as he turned into Oaklands Close. Halfway down the close, he saw a single fire appliance with its sidelights still on; parked just in front of that, a lone, unmarked police car, hazard lights on with two plain clothes officers sitting inside keeping warm. That's odd he thought, no hose lines or hose reels or equipment laid out and all the lockers were shut on the bright red Mercedes Atego. He drew up behind the fire truck and switched off the engine.

3

Around the same time, in a small office on the lower ground floor of the eastern wing of the Houses of Parliament, a telephone rang four times, stopped for a couple of seconds then rang four times again. In the low light of the office, barely illuminated by a single desk lamp, a glass was refilled to the brim with an expensive imported blend of Tennessee Bourbon, the bottle now down to just under half.

Relaxing back in his chair, Kyle Greenwood took another sip, the warmth and smooth liquid slid down to his stomach igniting a burning sensation throughout his body. He still couldn't believe his luck when offered this opportunity following a poor attempt to cheat a computer test while applying for a job. At first, he thought the head of security was going to beat him to a pulp but a couple of days later he received a call from the same guy with the strange accent offering him a short-term contract with massive benefits and he jumped at it, knowing full well most of it was far from legal but his role as a go-between wouldn't mean he got his hands dirty, well not too much anyway.

He picked up a mobile phone purchased two days ago from a small electrical shop in Oxford; the SIM card had been provided by his handler. There were only 5 numbers in the contact list, none with names, just symbols that looked like they belonged to the periodic table. His short text message read 'MANAGED TO CLEAN THE STAIN OFF THE CARPET, NO REPLACEMENT REQUIRED- Rn' the message was sent to 'Ar' from the contact list which he'd been given with specific orders to message completed only tasks to 'Ar' and any concerns to be sent to 'Ne'. The system for the organisation's communications at this stage of the operation was simple and clear, with information and tasks only, no questions to be asked and all phones to be checked every eight hours of their allotted time until further notice with no exception. He was told that all the key players of the group, during their three daily checks could receive information, tasks or confirm completion. This ensured no infiltration or breakdown occurred. Any alterations or changes would be made at the highest level only. The only issue that Kyle had with this was the requirement occasionally to use some poetic license to carry out his orders if he wasn't clear about what was expected, but so far, he had managed successfully.

He never expected a reply, it seemed that the only information he got was from 'Kr' and the other codes he was told he wouldn't need unless he hadn't heard from anyone during the time slots, in which case, he was told to message 'He' immediately with a simple 'Salus is silent' which he'd written on a slip of paper and kept in his wallet.

He switched off the phone, removed the SIM card and put everything in a small backpack where he wouldn't need to check it again for another eight hours. He emptied his glass, put on his jacket and after switching off the light, left the office heading for the deliveries entrance as his exit door. After signing out at the police checkpoint by the security gate, he crossed the road and headed for St James Park tube station to begin his routine trip back to a small, inconspicuous flat over an unoccupied shop on the edge of Oxford's city centre. The journey normally took about 90 minutes door-to-door but in the small hours of this morning, Greenwood was going to add thirty minutes of twists and turns, both on the tube and Oxford's streets, just to make sure he wasn't being followed, as suggested by his employer.

4

Bob grabbed his mug of tea, locked the car and turned towards the fire truck. Before he had made two steps, the front door of the truck opened and Steve Bryers jumped down with a torch in hand and without acknowledging Bob, started walking towards the front door of number 87. Bob followed in behind as if this was the norm, keeping about ten paces back, realising Steve was either making this formal or, as he suspected ensuring nothing looked out of the ordinary to something that obviously was. Bob played along by taking on the expression of a disgruntled officer having to attend a simple job at stupid o' clock in the morning and missing the warmth of his bed, for his extra 20% on-call allowance by walking slowly with an annoyed expression on his face.

Steve stopped about five feet from the front door, switched on the torch and pointed it at the top of the door, gesturing with his hands he spoke softly, not even turning his head away from the direction of the door,

"Follow my torchlight and nod a bit till we get inside."

The front door was being held in place by police tape that was wrapped around a small wall light and the letterbox, due to the damage caused by the fire crew forcing entry some three hours earlier. Steve unwound the tape, causing the door to swing inwards a few feet and again he played the torch around the frame and damaged areas, moving in a methodical dance which would appear to an untrained eye as the way it worked. Bob's responses of nodding and pointing were synchronized into the charade and the crew of the fire appliance sat motionlessly. This was nothing new to them, with the three in the back dozing, as the driver, Lou Dawlings, played Angry Birds on her phone while keeping radio watch.

The police however were not relaxing. They took turns to

constantly glance at the house for anything they thought didn't look right. It was a strange request that they had received direct from the Deputy Assistant Commissioner to proceed to the address and note anything out of the ordinary from the fire service crew and report directly back to her. Both had been in the Met for a few years and although their careers were not impressive by normal standards, they had somehow managed to find a protective hand from above and they were not about to jeopardise that relationship.

Pushing the door back and placing some damaged frame in place as a wedge, Steve moved into the hallway before speaking,

"Thanks, Bob, I'm sorry mate but I needed to share this with someone I trust."

"Sure, but what the fuck is going on with all the play-acting?"

Steve moved the torch around some more and went into the kitchen to replay the incident back to Bob.

"We got tipped out about 02:15 to a person's reported housefire from an abandoned call, so I'm thinking it's going to be a Micky."

Bob nodded, knowing that more often than not an abandoned call, especially in the small hours or at weekends, could be a malicious call as a prank or to move crews out of the area for other less salubrious reasons.

"So, anyway, we roll into the close, pulling up exactly where we are now."

Bob was listening to every word without interrupting; many years of experience had taught him to take in the whole story before asking questions or needing more details.

"The first thing that struck me as odd was that Plod got here only a few seconds after us."

Bob's reaction of surprise was the same as Steve Bryer's when he'd arrived at the scene hours before. Often police responses were thin at the best of times, if at all, especially at weekends due to all the other incidents they deal with as the drink-fuelled revelry unwound itself. And unless the incident commander requested them to attend specifically, in many cases this could take at best 15 to 20 minutes for a response.

"Anyway, there were no obvious signs of fire externally, so I started to assume just another malicious, but then we could hear a faint beeping noise like a smoke detector and peering through the letterbox, I could smell a faint whiff of smoke, so I ordered 2BA and a hose reel and we forced entry."

In between his description of the incident, Steve occasionally waved the torch around and made sure the light went down the hallway to the door to give the appearance of them still moving around inside.

"The crew very quickly cleared the ground floor and moved upstairs and on entering a rear bedroom, found a male approximately in his 40s, in the bed lifeless."

Steve went on to explain that the crew, realising the man was deceased left him in situ and checked the rest of the house for any other persons or fire and exited the building to pass on their findings to him. As were Brigade procedures, he had requested a Fire Investigation Team to attend next before entering the building with the police officers to begin his own initial investigation prior to their arrival. Continuing with the events of the incident, he made sure to keep the torch moving around.

"The ground floor was unaffected by any fire with only a small amount of smoke apparent which had drifted down the stairs, no sign of fire on the stairwell, again with very little smoke damage as I made my way up."

Bob had come across these types of incidents many times and often it was a small fire caused by kids playing with matches or a lighter in a bedroom and in most cases, extinguished very quickly.

"So, now I'm looking at a bedroom fire which seems not only to have developed quickly, sufficient to trigger a smoke detector but extinguished on its own just as quickly. Come and look at the room of origin."

They entered the rear bedroom and Bob turned to Steve with a puzzled expression.

"Where's the body?" he asked.

"The police arranged after the preliminary report by the FIT team to have the body removed."

"That's not what happens."

"I know, the FIT team based the death on smoking in bed with slow asphyxiation from smouldering bed linen."

"And?" Bob asked with an intrigued look on his face.

"And the police made a rapid decision that it wasn't a crime scene and after a quick phone call, the scene was closed down with a mortuary van turning up and the body removed."

Bob was surprised, even the body removal process could take a minimum of five to six hours to sort out; it seemed this was all done and dusted in record time. He was just about to make another comment when Steve's next words sent a shiver down his spine.

"The beeping smoke detector we found was placed on a chair seat just below the level of the bed; the police believe it was so he could smoke in bed without constantly setting it off and when I checked with control as to where the call came from, they said a male voice on an untraceable mobile stated he could see flames through the upstairs window and thought the house was on fire."

Bob let the statement sink in thinking that if the fire smouldered, there wouldn't have been any substantial flame, hardly even an orange glow. He paused for a few seconds then said,

"Let's get out of here, you get your crew back to the station and I will do some digging but as far as you're concerned, the incident is closed and don't speak to anyone about your findings. I'll see you Saturday for 18 holes."

They retraced their steps to the front door and exited the house. Bob fixed the door in a closed position while Steve got in the pump and left.

Bob walked over to the side of the police car and a window rolled down.

"What time is the SOCO turning up this morning?"

"Not happening, chief, because it was obviously accidental smoking in bed no further investigation is needed."

Bob never changed his expression, just shrugged his shoulders. "Fair enough," he said.

The officer in the driver's seat leaned across and looked through the window.

"Any issues? As the fire investigation team had already been, we didn't think we would see anyone else."

"It was only about the layout and materials involved; the incident commander wasn't sure if there was a need to check for a flawed manufacturing process with the mattress or the bed linen."

"And?" the driver spoke with an air of authority.

"Not from what I can see, just bad luck. I'll bid you a good morning, chaps."

He got back into his car and drove off, clearing about 2 miles north of Richmond Bridge then pulled over into a side street to make some notes in a small pocketbook.

5

The lift door opened on the third floor of a medium-sized purpose-built industrial unit tucked in the corner of a business park in Hounslow. Striding out with an air of arrogance and dressed in an Italian suit, the cost of which could have fed a family for a year, walked Emerson Jacobs. As he moved down the corridor of the building, he still allowed himself a warm feeling of achievement having acquired the perfectly-located building, redesigned the internal layout and had got all the work completed by a private overseas company with the funds from a business he had created from nothing, and even now was shrouded in mystery, evident by all the high-security fencing and what seemed like more outside video surveillance cameras than the Pentagon. It was the culmination of the last twenty years of his professional life dealing in computers and cyber-security and he now felt he was close to the pinnacle of his power.

The floors below to the ground were all open space office areas covered in computer terminals for the day-to-day work carried out by the small number of Emerson's minions, who were linked to companies of all types, globally. The only exception to the layout of the ground floor was a large conference room with four computer terminals arranged around a large square oak desk linked to a large single monitor used in training or for Emerson's purposes, as a way of testing potential whiz kids to hire or exploit.

As he walked towards his office located at the other end of the third floor, he passed through an open area measuring about two-thirds of the floor level which was divided by a thick, glazed wall and with banks of monitors and simple computer terminals virtually everywhere in the room, all of them switched off. The next section of the top floor before entering his office was a room with six 'super computers' as he liked to call them, three on each side. These were state-of-the-art individual systems linked into communication grids, satellites and pathways into governments and countries all over the world; each had its own clear working space separate from the others. These specific computers were hooked directly into a monster server located in a basement nearly as big as the building above.

He entered his office, sat down and looked at the two people he had just passed, working away at opposite ends of the bank of super terminals. He never acknowledged them as he passed, and they never flinched or were distracted by his presence. One was a young twenty-year-old Russian called Misha Kalenko, dressed in designer jeans and a Micky Mouse sweatshirt. He sat back, sipping a can of cherry coke and staring at the computer screen in brief pauses before leaning forward to tap the keyboard or move the mouse for a few seconds, then sitting back to take in the responses or actions and going again. The space around his terminal was littered with sweet wrappers, empty coke cans and a half-eaten pack of Jelly Tots, currently his staple diet.

All these things were the complete opposite at the other side of the workstations where a 35-year-old North Korean man sat in a smart suit and tie, jacket placed on the back of his chair. Although he was typing or moving his personal, wireless Lamborghini-shaped mouse at a quarter of the speed of Misha, his eyes flicked constantly around the screen, with an occasional pause for his brain to digest the information gathered and then he'd continue. Kim Son Tau or Kimmy as he was known sat with earphones blue-toothed to an iPod playing ACDC songs at nearly full volume to block out any distractions from his environment, mainly caused by the rustling of Misha's sweet wrappers or the sudden fizz of a can being opened every 30 minutes or so.

Emerson had no personal feelings for the two. They worked for him, he couldn't however deny the skills they possessed, which were something to behold, even by his standards. He knew their backgrounds, not just from what they had told him, but also from the information he had dug out from his massive computer systems and access pathways, which hunted the planet for anything he requested. There were still some areas he couldn't access, yet, but generally, the people and the equipment at his disposal gained him routes into many countries' infrastructures, finance and even some defence systems. Accessing any individual's personal information, which he often did to find useful things to blackmail or use as leverage on enemies or people he needed to control, was as easy for him as opening a packet of crisps.

He knew Misha was a product of Russian Intelligence, schooled in everything cyber-attack related, either dealing it out or stopping it coming in, whereas Kimmy was a master of viral software and the ways it could be used, like putting a spider in a web waiting for the fly to take the wrong turn, in a system that would sink deep into every file, code or drive and render you useless and at the mercy of the controller.

Emerson watched the pair for a couple more minutes before picking up a mobile phone from a desk drawer; on the back, it was marked with Ar. He tapped out a quick text message and hit 'send', then switched it off and replaced it in the drawer, alongside another five similar phones all with different taped letters. Turning back, he noticed on the main monitor in his office, a smartly-dressed couple coming into the reception area of the building.

6

07:08 and another early start of the week for Deputy Assistant Commissioner Georgina Williams of the Met who was tearing a strip off a Detective Chief Inspector over a surveillance operation that had ended badly with two Albanian enforcers managing to flee the country before a take-down and capture could be completed. The DCI was pleading his case that someone must have tipped them off, but this just appeared to make things worse.

Her eyes looked volcanic, and she concluded,

"You're a useless fuckwit, now get out of my office and make sure I have a full report on my desk by the end of the day!"

As he trudged out with his ears ringing, she followed just behind into the next room where her PA was typing away on a keyboard and keeping her head down.

"No calls for an hour unless someone blows up Parliament or the Commissioner wants to see me."

She turned back into her office, closed the door and sat back down, swivelling in her chair to look out of the window and stare across the London skyline. She closed her eyes and held a neutral expression; she contained the urge to smile thinking that tipping off the Albanian mob for a measly five grand was a bit low considering the workload now required to make the problem disappear. Just as she began to plan her response to the report, she heard a vibration in the bottom drawer of her desk. Glancing at the clock she became puzzled, it was an hour early.

She unlocked the drawer, took out the burner mobile and read the message: "ENSURE ALL OUTSTANDING LAUNDRY HAS BEEN CLEANED AND COLLECTED WITHIN THE NEXT 72HRS- He"

She understood what it meant and the need to take careful steps not to attract too much attention in carrying out what was required. She put the phone back and locked the drawer, before popping her head around the door and asking,

"Could you get hold of Area Manager Jeff Sykes of LFB to arrange a meeting to review cross-service arrangements for terrorist incidents?"

She knew Sykes would arrange a place away from prying eyes within the next day or two.

7

Bob pulled into the Brigade Headquarters car park at his normal Monday morning time of 8:15 and parked in one of the spaces reserved for Fire Safety Officers. Just as he was about to switch off the engine, he noticed a senior officer seemingly loitering around the entrance door to the main building. Pausing to check he had everything, he switched off the ignition and got out. He opened the back door and retrieved a small rucksack from the back seat, made eye contact with Jeff Sykes, locked the car and strode towards the entrance.

Sykes reacted to the eye contact, hurriedly reaching into his pocket and pulling out his mobile phone as if suddenly remembering he had to check something.

As Bob approached, right on cue Sykes replaced the mobile and used his ID badge to release the entrance door, then walked through, holding it open as if he had only just noticed Bob.

"Sorry, Bob didn't see you for a second."

Bob sped up a couple of steps as the door was being held for him.

"Morning how was your weekend?" Sykes added as Bob walked through.

"Fairly quiet Guv, just a fatal house fire at 3 in the morning, Sunday."

"I didn't think you were duty officer for the weekend."

"I wasn't but the incident commander was concerned about the plastic window trims being made from a non-standard material," he lied. "Because of my chemistry qualifications, he requested my attendance."

"Was there anything that we need to be aware of?" asked Sykes.

"No Guv, the stuff was all ok, just a different style of trim formed in a different process."

Sykes nodded in agreement as if he understood what Bob was talking about but in fact, he hadn't a clue. As if the final information was acceptable, Sykes turned and headed towards the lift without a further word. His destination was the upper floors where all the senior management resided but not the top three floors where the real power of the service sat. Sykes glanced very briefly back as the lift door opened but Bob had already begun his climb of the stairs, heading for the third floor and the sanctuary of his own office.

Bob sat down and took some time to digest what had just taken place.

Why did an Area Manager of Resources and Supply with no link to Fire Safety and a man who had never spoken to him before suddenly take great interest in his weekend activities? After about 30 minutes of his normal morning routine, checking emails, appointments or requests, he stuck his head out of the door.

"Janey, can you get the FIT reports for the weekend please?"

He went back to his desk leaving the office door open.

Jane Miller had worked with Bob for over 5 years and had known him for many more before that. She knew his routine better than he did himself and the reports were already on her desk ready for the call. As was customary, Jane made Bob a cup of tea in a large 'His Lordship' mug, walked in and placed the reports and tea on his desk.

"Thanks, Janey," he said as she left and closed the door.

Bob picked up the reports and knew that from a daily average of 500 to 700 calls the actual number requiring the FIT teams would be relatively small, although in this case, he was only interested in one report from the weekend.

8

There were 38 FIT reports from the weekend from the teams spread across the city. The usual mix, they ranged from a couple of insurance jobs that had been caught early enough to point the finger at the business owners, a jilted lover getting revenge without plainly thinking things through, a few burnt-out vehicles stolen or abandoned, and fires that had seemed odd at first and needed an explanation. Two-thirds of the way down the pile of reports, he found what he was looking for 'South Central FIT Incident Report Inc No 011215/03:07'.

He sat back in his chair and opened the file. The first few pages of the report were the incident log times from the moment a call was received to the closure and return of all appliances and officers allocated. All this information looked like the norm for such an incident with the first point of interest, as Steve had told him, being the time of arrival of the police. Although not impossible, it was just odd for a weekend when the police were normally kept busy with the social scene and all the problems that brought. Looking at the time they had arrived, it would have set a new world record and in Bob's mind, he could almost visualize the car following the fire truck all the way there from the moment it had left the station. As he moved to the officer-in-charge of the FIT team, to view his statement, an unfamiliar name appeared. He got up and walked to the door.

"Janey, could you get me the duty rotas of the FIT teams for the weekend just gone?"

He returned to his desk with a puzzled look on his face. He knew all the FIT team personnel well and had trained most of them himself, but this was a name he didn't recognize. Jane entered with the rota sheet.

"Grab a pew, Janey. Who is Station Officer Jack Drayton?"

"I think he's a jobsworth, normally found walking in the shadow of that new resources area manager."

"Syke's team?"

"Yes, why?"

"Just wondering why he would suddenly be leading a FIT team over the weekend when I haven't seen his name on anything previously or even know if he is qualified. Do me a favour Janey, without drawing attention have a look at the leave and sickness for that weekend and in particular what Andy Stewart was showing as."

Jane nodded and left. When she returned within 10 minutes, she looked puzzled.

"Sykes seconded Andy for the weekend, something to do with resourcing the FIT teams in a better structure and schedule."

Bob leaned back, put his hands behind his head and stretched his legs out, and as much as he thought he knew what was going on, he gave nothing away, simply saying,

"Must have swapped Drayton in at the last minute to cover it."

Jane looked up. "But the FIT teams are your responsibility to resource."

"Things must be changing in the upper echelons, Janey. Could you close the door on the way out and thank you."

Looking back at the report again, he noted that the information was thin with a brief statement from Drayton about the evidence of smoking in bed with smouldering bed liner apparent. There was a signature from him at the bottom of the report, co-signed by Detective Constable L Andrews who presumably was one of the officers sitting in the car at the incident scene.

"All very convenient," he muttered.

9

The sound levels began to increase with the squabbling voices at Prime Minister's question time; it was like a room of aristocratic head boys haggling over the price of a Cuban cigar worth £50 being sold to a street urchin for 50p, pointless but the argument needed to happen to justify their existence. Donald Lewis, MP and Financial Secretary to the Treasury was struggling to stay awake and kept checking his watch counting down to the next break so he could scurry off for a couple of cheap brandies in one of the thirty bars available in the building. Often his normal place to reside was the Bishop's Bar but today he knew he had to be at the Stranger's Bar. The recess was called and as if it were a factory floor or school closing for Christmas, the Commons Chamber emptied in a matter of seconds.

Lewis made his way to the bar where Kyle Greenwood was already seated with two glasses of brandy for the Secretary and a Bourbon for himself. As Lewis approached, Greenwood stood to great him as a sign of respect, not because he meant it but because it was about playing to the MP's ego to make him think he was the one in charge of things.

"Kyle, my dear boy, bloody good of you to double up the doubles!"

"I thought you may have needed it, Sir." The first brandy had gone by the time Kyle continued, "Minister, I have to report that things are moving along as planned and I have been tasked with finding out some more details regarding the processes in place at the Stock Exchange."

Lewis stared at his cradled glass without changing his expression.

"Do you need me to arrange another meeting with my contact?"

Kyle tried not to show his pleasure at winning so easily.

"If it's not too much trouble, Minister, that would be perfect," he smiled as if in awe of his master's skills. "Could it be organised this week, sir?"

"I will see what I can do," Lewis replied.

Kyle knew that the meeting could be sorted in the next 10 minutes but he had to play the part of a middleman who is led and not a leader.

Donald Lewis briefly thought back to how Kyle Greenwood had joined his staff after a party benefactor had suggested his services could enhance his standing within the party and the government. Initially, he had scoffed at the idea but over a short period of time, he became mightily impressed with the knowledge that was brought to him on other members, not only of the opposition parties but also his own. Information that was useful to persuade, alter or even destroy individuals who could stand in his way on route to a more powerful position. All that was asked in return was for information of financial details involving government policy and the Stock Exchange, with a particular interest in the Professional Securities Market or PSM.

Lewis downed his second brandy and stood followed in turn by Greenwood.

"Right Kyle, back to it, I will get the meeting details to you by the end of the day."

Kyle was about to say 'Thank you sir' but as he stood, Lewis had already left without a word of goodbye. Kyle Greenwood sat back down and sipped his bourbon, checked the time then sent a short message on his burner phone, switched it off and started thinking of the substantial pay off promised to him and what to spend it on. All he had to do was pander to a posh twit and leach information out of him.

10

Traffic seemed light for the early part of that Wednesday afternoon crossing Blackfriars Bridge and Jeff Sykes was happy the people on foot were low in numbers as well. He turned a few corners and found the small bistro off Whitefriars Street, at 14:33 it was only occupied by a couple of office workers grabbing a late lunch. Sykes entered with an A4 manilla envelope in his hand and headed to the far corner where Georgina Williams sat sipping tea and looking at an iPad. She didn't even acknowledge him when he sat down. Sykes glanced at the iPad screen expecting to see emails or documents but was surprised to catch a glimpse of what appeared to be an estate agent's site for properties in the Caribbean. As soon as she felt she was being scrutinized she closed the cover and looked up.

"Is the incident cleared from any further action?" she asked more as a statement than a question.

"Here is a copy of the report," replied Sykes passing her the envelope.

"The information contained is basic and minimal which will ensure that the coroner will agree with the cause of death being smoking in bed which will be ruled as accidental."

"And the operational crews attending have no issues?"

"Their reports and actions have been completed, in effect that is the file closed for them."

Sykes paused very briefly, and Williams was on it like a cobra striking.

"Yes?" she said.

"This report will still need to be checked by the Senior Fire Investigation Officer to question or confirm the conclusions and sign off as complete."

"I suggest you make sure that firstly, he files it with little examination and secondly that it disappears not long after." She spoke with a cold tone and her eyes burnt into his, this wasn't a suggestion it was an order.

She finished her tea, placed her iPad into a small rucksack, and as she rose to her feet, she glanced around the bistro gauging the scene for anything out of the ordinary, before returning her gaze back to Sykes.

"Keep your man close for use on another FIT team if required. I have been informed that there is potential for another small incident that may need the appropriate level of investigation."

It was Sykes's turn to look around the bistro, but his look was more of a nervous rabbit about to run across a motorway.

"I will need more details and-"

Williams immediately cut him off, "More information will be available if and when needed and will be exchanged in good time."

There was no goodbye and Sykes looked like a teenager having just been dumped by his girlfriend as Williams walked out of the door.

He ordered another coffee and a doughnut and sat thinking this isn't what he'd signed up for, covering deliberate fires wasn't supposed to have dead bodies in them. He knew the prize at the end was going to change his life, he just hoped he would be in the free world to enjoy it.

11

As routine for the start of a new week, Monday morning generally started with the two smartly-dressed people entering the building and reporting to Emerson, but today only one of them entered the office for an update with his master while the other, a confident-looking lady stood outside almost to attention with her back to the door.

"And you're sure he left the nightclub with her?"

Emerson didn't look up from the handful of still black images in his hands. The man standing in front of him was his chief of security, a title that screened much more of the duties he carried out for his master. Danny Van Bloche appeared to most as an uninspiring figure at 5'10", of medium build with a shaven head and goatee beard. At 48 there was nothing to highlight a risk or dangerous aura to this man. Dressed in a smart black suit but strangely sporting a bright orange shirt and green tie, people would struggle to take him seriously. In cases where people have crossed him or not properly read the signs, they found out to their cost, the kind of drive and purpose this man possessed. It was not uncommon in certain cases for people to mysteriously disappear having crossed him or tested his resolve.

Bloche had been born in Holland; his parents moved to South Africa when he was young, to an old family farm in the Western Cape where he worked during his teenage years. At 17, he joined the army and on operations during the 'Border Wars' attained promotion to the rank of Sergeant, but even this quick rise didn't fulfil his drive which led him to enrol in Special Forces training and gain a place among the 'RECCES'. For five years Bloche's abilities were honed and utilized for his adopted country, both in defence and aggression. It seemed his career was set for life until an unexpected turn of events led Emerson Jacobs to secure his skills for the company and his own personal use.

Emerson never thought back to that moment, but Danny knew very well that, had he not been in the wrong place at the right time on the night Emerson had taken a wrong turn and found himself in the Wolfgat Nature Reserve staring at a car blocking his way with three men armed with handguns and machetes, things would be very different today. The good luck for Emerson was the government's recent crackdown on violent crime and carjacking gangs, the bad luck for the three men, was that they had been followed by Danny as they came into his area of operation. There was no warning given; Danny took the first out with a stiletto knife, before swinging on the other two with a Heckler and Koch SFP9 pistol which dropped them before Emerson had even realised that he was there. From that day forward, he had made it his priority to recruit Danny to his inner circle.

Lifting his head from the photographs Emerson asked, "What do you know of the woman?"

"22 years old, studying law at the University of London, no criminal record obviously but she has been prominent in University Anti-Climate groups, some of which have been linked to Extinction Rebellion."

"Should we be concerned?"

"Only if information is passed outside of his normal cover."

"And your personal opinion?"

"Sir, my personal opinion doesn't enter into it, my professional opinion is it will only be a matter of time, short or long."

"Then let's remove that concern as soon as possible."

"Will that be all sir?"

"Yes, thank you, Danny. On your way out, ask Kimmy to come in."

Bloche nodded and left the door open as he went.

12

Troubling thoughts were not uncommon to Bob, he had often looked at reports for clues or links that may suggest a serial arsonist was at large or a scam being played out for financial gain, but this was different and after a week of deliberation he was at an impasse as to what he should do next. Logically, he knew that the incident had to be looked at again with senior management being involved but something just didn't feel right and for the first time in his career there was an unseen fear in him.

He waited for Jane to make the mid-morning cup of tea and as she delivered it with a couple of custard creams, he asked her to close the door and sit down.

"I need a favour when you pop out at lunchtime."

"Have you run out of Murray Mints again?" she asked jokingly, aware of Bob's fixation on consuming mints when thinking.

"No, all good. I still have two bags in the drawer."

"You must be cutting down."

"I need you to run an errand and deliver a note for me."

"Sure, where to?"

"Could you pop into Holborn Police Station and pass this in at reception?" He handed over a sealed envelope, marked '*FAO DCI George Calian- Personal*'.

"Is that the same George you worked with on the Kensington Gardens fires a few years back?"

"That's the chap."

"Wasn't he part Red Indian or something?"

"His family descendants were native Americans who settled

in London back in the 1800s after working on merchant cargo ships that travelled back and forth across the ocean."

As Jane got up to leave, Bob called her back before she opened the office door.

"Keep this to yourself, Janey, don't tell anyone where you've been, make something else up if asked." His expression was serious but also caring. He watched her place the envelope in her bag, grab her pink umbrella just in case and leave.

13

The nightlife in London never really stopped and there were always lively pubs and clubs open most nights of the week, especially through the summer months when the weather was good. Misha thought he was onto a winner that night in the club as he bought another round of vodka and red bull for the slim, very attractive and fit-looking brunette who had introduced herself as Naomi earlier in the evening. She had walked up to him at the bar asking if he'd seen a friend of hers who was supposed to be meeting her. What he would never work out was that under the black wig and make-up, Naomi was in fact Danny Van Bloche's Number Two, who often accompanied him to meetings with Emerson. She was a stunningly attractive blond normally, and as deadly as Van Bloche in every sense.

Naomi, or as she was better known, Danielle Keller had been working in South African Intelligence when she first met Danny and they clicked almost at once, becoming a formidable team working together. Trained in firearms and hand-to-hand combat, she was often underestimated by people in her company. She also suspected that her own peers in the intelligence unit were not totally convinced of her abilities when the high-profile threats were in play, so a move to the more lucrative business with Danny was a decision easily made.

"There you go Naomi, one more to see if your friend turns up."

"It's not looking likely at the moment though, is it?"

"I will have to do my best until then. So, what is it you do again?"

"I used to teach French when I left University but decided to make a change and moved into exporting artwork."

"Like Van Gogh or Renoir?"

"No, I look around the small galleries or even come across street artists, to buy and then export where the latest craving is for that style of art."

Misha didn't really understand but tried to maintain a look of interest. What he also didn't know about was the occasional small drop of Demerol that was being added to his glass whenever he went to the toilet. In the films they show tablets being dropped into a glass, fizzing then being drunk with an immediate reaction, but this wasn't how it worked, and Danielle was adjusting the levels carefully to ensure the right moment to intervene and have a compliant, manipulable Misha to remove from the club. She knew there was a support team nearby, possibly even someone keeping an eye on proceedings, but she was a talent and a force to be reckoned with and everything was planned with precision.

As Misha's words began to slur and he felt himself becoming unsteady, he suddenly felt relieved when Naomi said, "Let's get you safely home, I think you have had enough for the night."

His mind was scrambled but he felt his legs moving as they should, although quite slowly and he was thankful he was being guided by a slim lady with amazing strength. When he slumped into the back seat of what he thought was a taxi, he couldn't quite fathom why he was alone and didn't pick up on the woman who got into the front seat and drove off. Danielle would never use a taxi, it only added another witness to the task, so she had arranged for a contact to park a stolen black car just around the corner from the club at exactly 23:15 and walk away, leaving the keys concealed under the passenger floor mat. It was all about timing and proper planning.

By the time she had got Misha to the top corner flat, she was literally holding him up. His eyes were partially closed and she felt very thankful that the lift was working. The door was unlocked and as they stumbled through, Misha was unceremoniously dropped onto the floor. The flat looked like it had been decorated in the 1960s with dodgy-looking, flowered wallpaper everywhere and a scattering of old-fashioned dining room chairs around the traditional rectangular table with fold-out sides. The front door was closed and locked, and Keller went into the bedroom, while grunts and growling noises drifted out of Misha, face-down on the speckled brown carpet that probably hadn't been cleaned since England won the world cup in 66. The bed had already been arranged the night before with new bed linen dropped off by the support team to remove any other possible DNA getting dragged up if things went wrong. Danielle went back and got Misha to half-crawl while she half-dragged him into the bedroom and then bundled him onto the bed. She went back into the kitchen and in one of the cupboards retrieved a syringe and vial.

"Night Misha," she said with no emotion as the needle was gently pushed into his neck, nothing happened dramatically just the sound of breathing slowing down then silence.

The next part was the tricky bit and would need to be completed slowly and carefully resisting the urge to rush out. Placing an ashtray on the floor by the bed, she filled it with ash and cigarette ends from a plastic bag; then using a handful of turbo lighters began scorching the bedding. The hardest part was to get the room full of smoke without allowing a fire to start fully and it being discovered too soon. As the room began to smoke, Keller got it lower until the smoke haze was down to about four feet of gap from the floor.

Once she was happy the bedding wouldn't ignite, she crawled out, shutting the bedroom door and retrieving all the items that she had brought in, with the exception of the specially-designed smoke detector which she fitted into a bracket already on the ceiling outside the bedroom door. She then pressed the test button which made no noise but started a fifteen-minute count down prior to operation, set to keep sounding until either removed from its bracket or any button pressed which would silence it. She cracked the door to check the route was clear then headed for the stairs and exited within another minute. As arranged, another stolen car had been dropped at the junction of Catherall Road and Collins Road, the previous one having been removed and disposed of. She drove a few streets away, pulled over and switched on a mobile phone. She sent text messages to 'Ar' and 'Xe' 'ROOM READY FOR CLEARING-Kr'.

She sat quietly for just over ten minutes and after picking up the blue lights and seeing the outline of two fire appliances, she eased the car back out onto the road and headed west for two miles before abandoning the car in a pre-arranged spot for the support team to deal with and walked away.

14

George Calian was a 45-year-old veteran with over 25 years of service in the Met. He had served with some of the toughest units in London, including SO15 Anti-Terrorist and the Sweeny Flying Squad. As he had aged, he knew his body was not up to the manic pressures it was being exposed to and it became obvious it was a younger man's game, so he had decided to settle for a quieter role working out of Holburn Station as a Detective Inspector, dealing with the run of the mill crimes, murders and daily chores thrown his way.

Because he was old school, often he was only given the jobs nobody wanted or were not glamorous enough, basically as he had once said to his boss any shit job was dumped on him. What everyone did agree on was that he had a unique ability to get the job done when others couldn't. This was also apparent in him working alone mostly, as the methods sometimes applied could be bordering on 'a bit dodgy' as his DCI once told him. It wasn't that he broke the law, more like stretched it to suit or thought outside the box to get results. It was also well known that he could sit down for a pint with some of the city's top mob bosses and they would respect him professionally without threat or concern which had raised the odd question from the most senior officers in the Met, wondering if he was on the take. George needed them for their information as much as they needed him but there was never any money involved or bribery, just a mutual understanding of 'you scratch my back, I'll scratch yours'.

Finishing up a report over the successful busting of a recent car scam using fake taxis to overcharge people, often foreign tourists, by 'taking the scenic route' and doubling or tripling the fare in some cases, he got up from his desk to refill his mug with some black coffee. Next to a copier which looked more like some large grey and white plastic and metal magician's cabinet, in the corner of the main office was an old-style pigeonhole box system used for internal mail mainly but sometimes other private letters could appear as well. Looking over as he walked back with a freshly-filled cup and after being out of the office for a couple of days, he noticed some paperwork in his slot and wandered over to retrieve it. He returned to his desk and looked at a couple of memos of ongoing maintenance plans that the building was due soon, a note of open vacancies within the regional command and finally he opened the letter marked 'private/personal'.

'Hi George, hope all is well with you and you're not letting the kids get under your feet too much. Do you still drink in that iffy pub on a quiz night and if so, fancy a beer next week? to discuss the old days. Bob'

George let an amused grin appear on his face at the kid's comment which he knew was referring to all the other younger officers in the command. He sat down and put the letter in his jacket pocket.

15

The Lord Nelson on the corner of Manchester Road in Millwall was not a pub Bob would frequent as a habit due to its distance from his home and office, but he knew this was where George found sanctuary from other officers or management and the term 'local' meant pretty much that; only acceptable clientele and the well-behaved were afforded refreshment. Unless you were with someone known or who knew you, you could be scanned, vetted, and monitored with any result from being bought another beer on the house, asked if you want to 'marry my daughter' and accepted, or required to leave faster than a bullet train.

The quiz started at 8 pm on Wednesdays. As usual, Bob entered seven minutes past and hoped George was already seated somewhere. He wasn't disappointed. As he walked to the bar, he noticed George tucked in a corner, alone and half-way through a pint of Guinness. Bob ordered two more pints of the same and as he walked over, he felt the locals' eyes and then the tension eased as they saw where he was headed.

"There you go George, good to see you again," he said putting the glasses down on the table and sitting opposite.

"Long time Bob, good to see you again; the family all good?" he asked, extending his hand to shake Bob's.

"All good thanks."

"I'm assuming this visit is not official judging by your lack of detail in the note and the mention of the kids."

"I couldn't be more precise; I wasn't sure who may have got a look at the note before you got it and I also know this place wouldn't have been picked up from the quiz night reference by your work comrades."

"And you knew I would be here on time?"

"Hoped you would be, more to the point."

"So, tell me, Bob, what's got you so spooked?"

The pub only had its regulars playing the quiz at that time which amounted to about fifteen or sixteen people and George had picked a table at the other end of the main lounge bar where any conversation could be had with no ears listening in. Bob took a big gulp of Guinness and proceeded to talk through all the strange goings on from the beginning; the call to attend the fatal fire, Police responses, the FIT team report and the odd questioning from Jeff Sykes.

George absorbed all the information and then asked,

"What can you tell me about the two police officers in the car at the scene of the fire?"

Bob thought back and described them as best he could remember at the time, then dragged up a name from the FIT report which had a police officer counter signature that was thankfully not a scribble.

"The copper's name in the initial findings' remarks was a DC L. Andrews."

"Lenny Andrews I would say from your description, he is one of Witch Williams' lap dogs."

"Who's Witch Williams?"

After explaining the inner workings of the Met rank structure and linking Lenny Andrews and most likely his sidekick Chris Daniels to the fire, with Williams' possible involvement, it was apparent to George that whatever Bob was mixed up in wasn't beneficial at this point to shout out about.

"First things first, Bob don't put your head up above the parapet and keep everything to yourself for now."

"Thanks, George, on that note I'll get another couple of pints."

Bob sat in silence for about ten minutes while George spun

the details around in his head, muttering about the incident and any relevance to Williams. It wasn't being done for Bob's benefit, but it seemed that George was replaying things back and forth and throwing in other possible reasons or actions.

He suddenly snapped out of it and looked at Bob.

"Right, what you do is nothing for now and let me see if I can find out anything from my side. It may be the guy involved is known in criminal circles, hence the actions taken but if not, and they get wind someone is looking in, that could be a tad risky."

"What if I need to get you, or you me?" Bob asked.

"Unless I get a message to you, which I can, don't try to contact me and be here next week at the same time; and Bob, if I'm not here, leave straight away with a packet of crisps or peanuts."

Bob looked at him with a quizzical expression.

"Got to have a reason for popping in."

George watched Bob leave before ordering another beer, then sat down to think through the next steps and how best to approach things without drawing attention to himself which wasn't going to be easy if done officially.

16

"So just to confirm it, Edward, the securities market is not a regulated market but is a specialist security one let's say, for example, depositary receipts."

"Yes, that is a simple summary."

"But the level of protection applied is the same as all the Stock Exchange protocols?"

"Generally, yes, but with also a few additional ones as the interest in this market includes organisations with non-specified methods of accruing finance."

At this point, Kyle Greenwood became as focused as a hawk above a field mouse.

"Added levels of monitoring, pass keys or access requirements?" Greenwood asked.

"We have the normal cyber protections in place such as firewalls, but because this market is a favourite with foreign powers, there were a few modifications post 9/11 and 7/7."

"You have modified the exchange?"

"No, MI5 and MI6 Cyber Task Forces are the main overseers to the main security monitoring, but we introduced a couple of key partners into the system with checks as support with a reciprocal protocol in place."

"Checks? I don't fully follow."

"I would have thought the Right Honourable Mr Lewis would be aware of these things in line with his position."

"He has a rough awareness but wants to review things a little before looking at approaching the PM with possible funding to improve security further," Greenwood lied.

"I think the Exchange is nailed up pretty tightly with what is now in place, we have something called the 'Outer Cerberus Lock' which is monitored by MI5 and the CIA like a front door access key and totally undetectable until you hit it."

"I get that, presumably because of the link to the New York Exchange, but you said, key players?"

"In the server system for this market, NAICHO have piggy-backed a virus detection system known as the 'Jorogumo Net'. "

"Cerberus I've heard of but Jorogumo, what's that?"

"I don't know the full story but what I found out by googling it, is the Jorogumo was a mythical Japanese shape-shifter that would often take the shape of a woman spider that would ensnare and devour, so apply that in computer systems I suppose."

"I am a little surprised that the Japanese Intelligence Agency are linked in."

"They have a better handle on the Asia crime scene than just about anyone else, apart from China, who are generally involved with some of the issues we worry about and as part of the top three markets the Tokyo Exchange was worth collaborating with, financially-speaking."

As Edward Collingwood, a descendant of Admiral Collingwood of Nelson's time finished his explanation to Kyle Greenwood, he was totally unaware that the last 37 minutes of their meeting had been recorded on three different devices in the office where Kyle based his quieter activities. No Bourbon bottles in sight, just a tray with a plain white teapot, two cups with saucers and a small plate of biscuits which had not been touched.

"Thank you for this Edward, I am sure that Donald will pass on his thanks to the right people in the right places."

"Thank you for the tea. Which is the easiest way to get out of this place?" Edward said as he stood and picked up his coat, briefcase and traditional black umbrella which he carried not for the rain in the summer months, but as a symbol of his standing.

Kyle escorted him to the same exit he always used to avoid as many people as possible in the building and hurriedly returned to his office to make a report.

17

It was Jane who highlighted another FIT Report to Bob that morning, even before his daily chores had begun.

"It's on the top of the pile, another Jack Drayton incident."

"Have you looked at the report, Janey?"

"No, I just noticed the fatal flat fire in the log and checked the OIC of the FIT Team."

"Ok, thank you. Could you close the door on your way out please?"

As with the previous report, the information contained in the pages was thin with a cause put down to smoking in bed. He noticed the police signature as DC Daniels which was the other name George had told him and the sidekick to DC Andrews. Bob assumed that they had both attended again but switched signing the report so as not to draw suspicion. Bit late for that he thought to himself.

Working through the report, again he noted the lack of information and a simple explanation that had been put down for a cause of death, asphyxiation from smoking in bed. The age of the deceased had been put as unknown but a young male with no formal identification available at this time. Again, the lack of detail about the deceased should have rung alarm bells with the police and a full investigation requested purely on ensuring this person hadn't been logged on any missing lists or even any criminal background history. The scene should have started as a crime scene at the top level and then dropped down the pile as information was confirmed.

He took out some key pages, photocopied them and placed them in his briefcase. He spent the next couple of hours writing up reports on each of the files and passed them back to Jane.

"Nothing unusual, Janey. File these as normal and pass the stats up to management."

As he spoke, he gave Jane a look that told her the opposite and she knew he was like a dog with a bone and would run things down to a conclusion, one way or another.

He finished his morning's work and decided to use the headquarters' gym for an hour. With his ear buds in and his iPod on, he selected his chill playlist and began an hour of walking on the treadmill at a brisk 6.2 km with Sinatra's Fly Me To The Moon as the opening track. He mulled everything over in his head and was hoping George Calian would be quizzing again tomorrow night and he knew he had to get a look in a certain flat in Highbury New Park as soon as was safely possible.

18

Kimmy's expression never altered as Emerson fed him the new information about the Cerberus Lock and the Jorogumo Net. He made a few notes on a pad and when the conversation was over, just replied,

"It is doable sir, but will take time."

Emerson knew time was not something he could spare but also knew he had no alternative but to push on.

"Keep me updated and if you need any encouragement, how about 100k extra if it can be done within 2 weeks?"

There was no change in the North Korean's expression, he just turned back to the keyboard and started his work again.

Emerson walked into his office, sat down and asked his reception desk to contact his security manager and send him up as soon as possible. He always knew that achieving his plan was going to take time but with the untimely problems of recent weeks, with the nosey cleaner they had employed and the loose-living Russian, he was unhappy as to what problems may be getting raised with other authorities or forces out of his control.

Danny Van Bloche entered within two minutes of being requested. There was no sign of running in or responding like a trained pet but a punctual walk that said ready for instruction.

"Danny, I have some work for you and Danielle."

"Sir?"

"I want you to review the recent problems and ensure there are no loose ends beginning to show. I also want you to look at the table properties and any links to the main elements."

"Yes, Sir."

"Any areas of concern you find, resolve them and don't let anything lead back to this office."

"Does that include full action on the main elements if required?"

"Yes, but I want any information squeezed from them if that turns out to be the case."

"Of course, Sir."

"And Danny, don't use any outsiders."

Danny just nodded and left.

19

Bob parked his car at Millwall Fire Station again and let the Duty Officer of the watch know he was leaving it there for about an hour and began walking the just over a mile route down Westferry Road and entered the pub just before 8 pm. As before, George was in the corner away from the locals who were getting ready for the quiz. This time though there was already a Guinness on the table for him.

"Cheers, George," Bob said as he sat down.

George raised his glass and took a large gulp, glanced around the pub just to make sure he hadn't missed anything earlier.

"Well, you were right to flag it up, but I'm not quite sure yet what shit storm you've fallen into."

"Tell me something I don't know."

"The body at Oaklands Close has already been cremated and all the paperwork completed, no next of kin identified, apparently. My darker sources tell me he was a Moroccan illegal who worked as a cleaner for a company called 'CleanFact' which specialises in factories and industrial units."

"Well, that's one of the problems cleaned up, literally," Bob added with a sarcastic smirk.

"I couldn't get much information from the person I spoke to, Bob, but I want to take a closer look at that company's unit."

As George took another mouthful of Guinness, Bob pulled out some folded-up paperwork from under his jacket.

"Any chance I could join you and if we have time take a look at this place as well?"

He handed over some of the photocopied report he took on Monday morning which referenced the second fatal fire very much like the Oaklands incident.

"I see that the blue numpties were there again as well," as George had labelled DCs Daniels and Andrews.

"You'd almost think they were jinxed," Bob replied.

George focused on the report and looked up a few times to glance around the pub. Occasionally he would raise his glass, take a big gulp and just stare for a few seconds at the bar before returning to the report. If the main door opened or closed, he would lower the report to his lap and narrow his vision looking like a tiger searching his prey. Only locals came and went and after about five minutes he gave the report back.

"I would put money on it that the scene there is going to be similar to the first, looking at this report and your detail of the Richmond job."

"That's why I want to take a look sooner rather than later," Bob said emptying his glass and getting to his feet to get another couple of pints. He returned a few moments later with two more full glasses and sat down.

"What we do know so far is that there are some pretty influential players involved and they may be top of the pile, but if they are cogs in a more complicated machine, this monster could be quite destructive."

George was looking at Bob as he spoke with an expression of *do you really want to do this?*

"I can't turn my back on this, George, I just don't know who to trust yet."

"Right, here's what we do, tomorrow night at 11.30 I am going to drive down your road and stop two houses further down on the opposite side of the road and you're going to walk out and get in."

"What do I need?" Bob asked.

"Dress in black from head to foot. I will have everything else you need."

George paused for a drink and then added in a serious tone, "Bob, if I drive down and don't stop at 11:30 then assume I am being tailed and I'll come back at 12:30."

"What happens if it's my house they're watching?"

"In that case, you won't see me. Stick to your daily routine, and we will have to have another beer next week, but I'll be in touch if that happens, somehow."

20

There was no commotion; George managed to drive by and park two houses down, as he had said, and Bob walked out and got in. The car was a dark blue Renault Megane which had its fair share of small dents and scratches, the sort of damage you constantly pick up at a Sainsburys' car park thanks to people pushing trolleys down the side or up against your boot when loading their shopping.

"Before you ask, I've borrowed it from a private source."

George didn't look at Bob but knew what was going through his mind.

"We certainly don't stand out," he replied.

"It's all legal and won't raise any flags to other agencies or ping up any problems on any ANPR Cameras."

They drove on in silence for 35 minutes before George pulled over into a parking space along Barlbary Road, North Kensington. They sat for about 15 minutes while George surveyed all the movement around their general area and any vehicles passing them.

"Right, put these on and when we get out, we are going to walk back up the road and just past Barlbary Gardens, we will be making a turn."

George passed Bob an orange hi-vis surcoat with 'Network Rail' on and a bright yellow hard hat.

"Not very conspicuous though," Bob said.

"Not yet, but the idea is not to stand out by standing out," George replied.

They got out and walked about 200 yards up the road before George turned up a small footpath which led to some scrubland;

then they found themselves walking along a track parallel to the railway line. The track wasn't well lit but there was just enough light from the side of the railway to show them the route. George slowed and told Bob that in another 50 yards they would divert into the Little Wormwood Scrubs Park and remove all the hi-vis gear and take another direction.

As they entered the park, George waved Bob to follow him to a clump of hedges and trees where a small rucksack had already been hidden the night before by George with all the tools he needed.

"Stash the hi-vis in the black bin liner and we will retrieve it on our way back. And, Bob, when we get in there just in case, no talking just signal, point or wave. I am pretty sure some of these places are using sound recorders for their inner offices and CCTV externally."

"How are we getting by the CCTV?" Bob enquired before they set off again.

"I have a small box that will scramble their system, but I don't want to be in the building any more than about 30 minutes tops, or sooner if we find something."

They slowly moved through the park, hugging the tree and hedge lines. Occasionally George would stop for a few seconds to look and listen before moving on.

They found themselves in the corner of the park by a wall with savage-looking wire, spikes topping it, that ran the length of where the industrial units were. Bob looked a little concerned but an image of ripping his manhood apart soon subsided as George led him to a spot where scaling the wall was so simple it was laughable, how any site security hadn't picked it up before was unbelievable.

On the perimeter wall for the industrial units, the site owners had provided a smoking shelter which obviously had been positioned after the wall and its obstacles were constructed. Amazingly, they had somehow managed to place the cover of the shelter to overhang the wire and spikes, from the park side. George backed Bob against the wall and got him to provide a foothold and lifted him up and onto the corner of the shelter. It was a flimsy structure but by staying at the side, it would take their weight easily. George positioned his boots carefully on the top of the wire and leaned over to take Bob's hand and pull him up. They shuffled along the shelter and thanks to the chairs left for people to sit in comfort on their fag breaks, they stepped down without making a sound. It would also aid them on the way back.

Bob never asked George how he was going to get into the unit but was surprised when they headed for the main entrance door. The area around the industrial units was partly illuminated by floodlights on the buildings, but some were so thickly covered in bird droppings, and a few were not even working, that the effect was to give off a slight orange glow around some of the buildings, with some areas darker than others. In one such shadow, George slowly moved, took the rucksack off his back and removed some tools that resembled a small crucifix with teeth and a thin, flat bar. Putting the rucksack back on he looked at his watch and went to work. To Bob, it seemed like minutes, but the door was open in a matter of seconds, they moved in, and George closed the door. Bob held his breath expecting an alarm to sound but nothing, not even a pre-alarm waiting for a code to be entered to stop the sudden screams of panic.

George took out a couple of small, pencil-shaped torches that focused the light into a small but powerful glow, enabling them to move safely without tripping over things and gave one to Bob. They moved through another door into an open space that had a large roller shutter door, used to load and unload vans. Around the main unit floor area stood badly-made DIY wooden racking and shelves with containers of cleaning liquids, various-sized dust sheets, covers and brooms, brushes and mops. At the end of the racks was an area where assorted electrical appliances were kept such as floor cleaners and industrial vacuums. On the opposite side from the racking and equipment were a couple of small offices made from stud work partitioning, one door was open to a small room with a table, a couple of chairs, a microwave and a kettle on a worktop with a small sink. This was obviously the rest area which also had a single toilet off from it. The other room became just as obvious to him as the office and George went straight to it, and opened the door which thankfully was unlocked removing more time-wasting gaining access. This room had a small desk with a rather worn office chair behind it and in the corner stood a couple of locked filing cabinets that grabbed his attention and he moved straight to them.

George took a couple of tools from the rucksack to quickly gain access.

In one of the cabinets the paperwork held details of deliveries and suppliers, the other was what George was after. In the second drawer down, he found a couple of Manila folders with 'Current Contracts' and the first one he looked at gave details of the company name, time allocated, what was required with the number of personnel and frequency required. He took both large folders put them in his rucksack and motioned for Bob to follow him. They retraced their steps to the door and George opened it about an inch and listened for a few seconds before increasing the gap to allow them through. He made sure the door was locked and they moved back into the shadows before using the chairs up onto the smoking shelter to get back into the park. The tension eased from Bob a little as he thought that's one down one to go.

21

Time was on Danny Van Bloche's side as he drove past the industrial units, just after 1.40 in the morning with the knowledge that all these particular units only operated in the daytime hours, but he still glanced down between each unit to check if there was any sign of activity. Turning around, he came back, slowed down and stopped. He switched off the lights and sat in the dark watching the units, the access roads and any movement his brain interpreted, be it animals, trains or people which at this time were virtually non-existent.

After 15 minutes, without turning the lights on, he reversed the car back into a spot by a large group of skips and sat and waited for another 5 minutes. He knew that some units would have CCTV, but chances were they wouldn't be covering the back ends of the units and if the business was that valuable, there were likely to be cameras inside and a decent alarm system which he knew wasn't going to be the case for this cleaning company which was one of the cheap ones in the area. He had known businesspeople like this and knew that all the profits would be spent on the owner with the overheads barely being covered and wages would most likely be the minimum wage at best with occasional small cash payments for illegal immigrants or underage workers.

Slowly and as quietly as possible, not to make a noise but to ensure his senses could still pick up any noise or movement he got out of the car and closed the door. He moved to the boot which had been popped as he reversed back to the skips to cover the noise and retrieved a thin, flat bar with a small jemmy tool and some wire. A few other fine precision tools were in the side pockets of his black combat trousers, should he need them. He paused for a couple more minutes to take in the surrounding area for any sounds and moved along the rear of the units, hugging close to them in the shadows. He paused at the corner of the line of units to take in the area again but only noticed in the distance a couple of rail workers in hi-vis jackets walking away down a track running parallel to the railway line.

He found a side window into the unit and got to work which from his experience was going to be straightforward, based on the cheap double glazing and poor plastic frosted covering to stop people looking in. The window opened a little and then caught and it took a few more seconds for his gloved hands to find the catch that enabled the window to open fully and allow him access. He pushed the window back and with a small red pen light looked around. He was in the office and looking around he saw some filing cabinets which were locked which although would not take too much to pick would prolong his time in the unit and he didn't want to spend it looking through files. He moved out into the main unit area and found the original fire alarm panel which had been isolated from the mains and the battery disconnected, often another way of keeping the bills down without the need to test and maintain at the owner's expense.

Moving back, he located some flammable cleaning liquids kept in 5-litre plastic containers. He took a couple of containers and carefully poured them into gaps and holes at the top of the filing cabinets and was rewarded with small puddles seeping out of the bottom of both which confirmed the solution had soaked down into the files. The nearly empty containers were replaced back in the storage area, and he picked up another which he poured outwards from the rack towards the electrical appliances, including three battery leaf blowers that were on charge on a small bench. The next step was to build a path to the office with items that would catch fire quickly and lead the flames up to the filing cabinets but not attract too much suspicion. The rest of the unit might be saved but only if detected by a passer-by or if an adjoining unit's alarm system was activated.

His final task was the trickiest and just before that he went back to the office and opened the window fully, moved back to the storage rack of cleaning fluids and each container he had used he laid on the side and loosened the lids enough for a liquid to slowly disperse but not empty out instantly. The final act was to pull a plug out of the socket near the floor that was charging a leaf blower, break the cover to expose the wires and plug it back in at which point he checked that the flammable liquid was below the socket, and now the moment to test his nerve. From his leg pocket he took out an extendible pointer used in schools and conference meetings to tap the boards or walls, which extended to 6 metres; he opened it fully and at the end was a small bud of cloth which had been dipped in paraffin with a small plastic bag wrapped around to keep it damp. He took off the plastic cover and ignited it and from a distance, he placed the flaming spot above the liquid just below the socket. It was not an exact science when the liquid would ignite but from previous experience, he knew that there was a brief moment when the ignition point would react and that was the moment he would need to move. The reaction didn't take long, and Van Bloche moved quickly, swiftly exiting the window and glancing back briefly to see the conflagration had taken as he'd planned. He closed the window but although he knew the fire would take a firm grip quickly, he paused at the corner of the unit for around ten seconds to check the surroundings. It was pointless to strain too hard to hear anything because he was aware of the crackle of flames beginning to eat their way into the unit. Retracing his tracks, he got in the car and drove off without any lights for the first 50 yards and at a steady speed.

22

Bob and George had returned to the car in their hi-vis jackets and drove off straight away without lingering in the street to discuss things. As they headed back across London, Bob didn't need to give the address for the flat, George had told him he'd already looked at the access and parking places so as not to draw too much attention when they arrived in the area by having to drive around.

They drove for about forty minutes then turned down Stoke Newington Church Street, then into Clissold Park and stopped along a lane reasonably covered by trees and hedges.

"After we exit the park, we will be visible and this time dressing as rail workers won't wear it and looking like ninjas all in black is likely to draw attention as well," said George.

Bob looked at George with an expression of 'are you for real' as from a bag behind his seat, George had withdrawn two green bomber jackets and what looked like king-size white baseball caps.

"I hope you're not expecting me to strut along and keep calling you bruv?" Bob said.

"Don't worry, we don't need to claim the hood as long as we don't get fronted up by the local massive."

George was looking at him with a big grin on his face.

They never saw any people of interest on the short walk to the block and as they entered the stairwell, George told him that he would get Bob in and then wait outside, covering the landing for no more than about fifteen minutes before coming back.

George picked the lock to the flat door and opened it slowly, there were no sounds, no feeling of occupation and a faint whiff of smoke seeping out of the wallpaper.

"15 minutes Bob, it doesn't pay to hang around too long."

Bob nodded and entered the flat. He closed the door and with his torch low, started a short circling movement around the room taking in the stains on the floor, some water and some other liquids he didn't really want to think about. The smoke-stained wallpaper gave off an image of a fire that was not very hot and the barrier or fire plane hadn't dropped much before extinction. The flat seemed sparsely furnished, apart from a mouldy-looking brown striped sofa and matching armchair, some dining room chairs with a cheap plywood dining table in front of them. It was either used for dodgy dealings as Bob always called them, drugs or prostitution normally, or sometimes a stop-off point for illegal immigrants to hide out for a few days before being moved on.

On entering the bedroom where the fire according to the report had started, he noticed the bed pushed up against the wall in the corner with various charred areas along the sides and at the corners of what was once a white mattress, now heavily stained with various yellowing splashes and blotches. There were no bedding or blankets which he thought had probably been moved outside by the fire crew when they were damping down the scene and subsequently taken by the local council refuse team later or at the conclusion of the incident. He looked in the kitchen lastly and noticed all the cupboards were completely empty which in his mind was unusual; there was always something left, out of date beans or soups, a mouldy box of crackers or at least a packet of uncooked rice or pasta but nothing and he couldn't swear it, but the inside of the cupboards looked like they had been wiped, with very little dust or cobwebs evident.

He walked back to the front door and opened it to peek through and as he did so, George spoke quietly from the stairwell door just along the landing, telling him to come on out.

As they made their way back through Clissold Park, George spoke first,

"Was it worth the visit?"

"Whoever was in that flat didn't die from smoke inhalation unless they had been standing on a stool to keep their head up in the smoke. Also, someone thought the inside of the kitchen cupboards needed cleaning when everything else in the place was a shithole," Bob replied.

As they reached the car and removed the bomber jackets and baseball caps which almost made Bob feel like he had returned to his own timeline, George looked across the roof as he opened the door.

"I reckon it may be worth looking into the owner of that flat and I'll work my way through these files from the cleaning company."

They drove in silence as Bob worked the scene in his head and the type of fire evidenced by the visible signs. George drove down the road and went back around again as he checked that nobody was monitoring Bob's house or that there were people sitting motionless in cars. He slowed and went two houses past Bob's and stopped. As Bob got out, George said,

"Beer tomorrow, same place?"

Bob nodded and left as George drove off.

23

A normal steady sequence changed as the keys were pressed on the keyboard and they appeared to slow from the usual rhythmic dance and Kimmy's eyes seemed to enlarge before his brain had deciphered what he was seeing. He glanced around to look at Emerson who was on a mobile phone, and when Emerson looked back at Kimmy, he hung up, got up from his desk and walked towards him.

"I believe, Sir, I have found out how to bypass the 'Cerberus Lock' without any flags being raised."

"Can you try it out on the target?" Emerson asked in a slightly excited tone.

"I do not think that would be a good idea at this time, but I could try something similar on another high-profile system which if successful would 99% prove we have a way in."

"Do you have a sacrificial site and what do you intend to do?"

Kimmy looked up to the ceiling and closed his eyes for a few seconds then looked back at Emerson.

"The Vatican City has a banking system that for over hundreds of years has been shrouded in controversy and mystery, it was even rumoured that the Mafia had used it for money laundering which the church turned a blind eye to for some reasonable recompense."

Emerson nodded he had heard the stories as well.

"Well, the thing is the Sicilian families provided funds to upgrade part of the accounts system in the early 80s which with the improvements in technology and certain bright individuals in the cyber business, the Mafia still managed to hold a single account buried deep within, with a rumour that it has billions in it called Deus Aurum or God's Gold."

"Dollars?" Emerson asked.

"I believe it was Swiss francs so they could move it easily into the Swiss banking system before removing or adding."

"So how is this going to be a similar trial?"

"In training with the cyber force in Pyongyang, we were all asked to select a task from a given list to try and break into and exploit, corrupt or steal from."

Emerson became intrigued enough to pull up a chair and sit down.

"The list included the normal ones, FBI or CIA Headquarters, MI6 and various other military branches of the major countries opposed to our glorious leader's reign. However, also included were a few rather unusual ones, the French wine producers' information on Beaujolais release dates or Japan's whaling fleet scheduled areas of operation, but another colleague saw The Ezra Gateway."

Emerson had been raised with some Christian background as a child, but his knowledge was limited to Moses, a few disciples and turning water into wine, so it wasn't unexpected when he replied,

"Ezra isn't something I can recall from my youth."

Kimmy was sure most wouldn't have heard of Ezra, let alone the gateway.

"The quick version is that God inspired the King of Persia to commit a member of the Jewish community to carry out a mission, which led to three successive leaders completing three missions."

"Go on," Emerson replied.

"The first was the rebuilding of a temple, the second to purify the Jewish community and the third was to seal the holy city behind a wall. The Ezra Gateway uses these three principles in its simplicity but as my colleague found out, simple wasn't even close."

"Were the three principles sub-routed or standalone barriers?"

"The thing is he never got past the first part without triggering a flag which not only blocked him but also managed to identify the system where it had come from and allowed counter access into the server he was using, and it installed an expanding concrete virus basically setting everything in the server and linked systems solid."

Emerson knew all about these viruses and had even used them on occasion, but he'd never known of any big operators or agencies being caught out by them.

"Anyway, the senior officials weren't too impressed with the guy when it started and I never saw him after that day, although I did hear that all the linked equipment he had used, and the server, had to be destroyed."

"What sort of stuff was lost?" Emerson asked.

"Luckily, of the servers we used in initial training and practice, hacks only kept small unimportant details, but the loss of all the linked equipment was in thousands."

"So, what do you make of this Ezra Gateway?"

Kimmy began to explain the principles of both the Cerberus and Ezra systems and how they would trip up hackers, jumping without analysing each move before physically taking the next step, then added,

"I think the mistake he made was he thought that the three steps were individual ones, but as the book stated, they were three missions, so I think there are multiple tasks to each step which are interlinked but not obviously apparent."

"And if you don't have the correct sequence, any step in the wrong direction will create a flag," Emerson responded.

"Yes, but I think what I have created will ghost each step before actually stepping forward which will avoid a flag being triggered."

"What about the individual missions, like the book says?"

"What I believe my program will do is locate the mission link as it ghosts through the steps which should in effect let me in without even being noticed."

"When will you try it and how long will it take?"

"I'm going to piggyback a server then redirect via another somewhere near the Vatican City. So, if this fails, I will clear this point long before it can be traced. It will take me about an hour to upload my program then all being well, I would say to get all the way into Deus Aurum Account will take between four and six hours."

Emerson stood and headed back to his office and Kimmy returned to his screen, put his earbuds in, hit play on his iPod and began tapping the keyboard again.

24

That evening, as Bob entered the Lord Nelson, he noticed the normal corner was taken by three people, but he continued to the bar. The barman had started pouring a couple of pints of Guinness as he walked in and passed them to him.

"George is in the beer garden and these are taken care of."

Bob thanked him and went out into the beer garden where George was sitting on a bench with a few pieces of paper in front of him. There was nobody else in the garden but as was normal, George had positioned himself in a spot to see all around, and was able to notice anybody taking a keen interest in them should they arrive.

"Thanks, Bob," as another pint was put down in front of him.

Bob took a seat opposite and took a decent sip from his glass as George began,

"Firstly, that flat in Highbury is down as a vacant possession with the local authority, so nothing to help us there, and it's probably just been left to rot until someone made them an offer which has allowed all sorts to use and abuse it."

George then passed him a couple of the bits of paper that had been in front of him.

"These are the receipts of cleaning work carried out between January and April this year for some industrial units scattered around London."

Bob glanced at a list, but nothing stood out to him, and he looked up at George.

"Don't worry, I was expecting that look." He passed him another sheet.

"Look halfway down in the month of June and tell me what you see?"

Bob followed the list down and without looking up said,

"One of the units cancelled its contract on June 17th."

"And when did that fire in Richmond happen?"

"June 19th."

George passed him another piece of paper.

"This is a copy of a Coroner's file note for the death of the guy at Richmond." George then passed him another piece of paper which looked like a poorly-scripted employment sheet and added, "The guy found dead in the Richmond fire was also the same guy who did some late-night cleaning at this unit up until June 17th, the same unit that suddenly cancelled its cleaning contract the same day."

Bob felt a knot turning in his stomach and looked at George and said,

"That cleaning company's unit went up in smoke in the early hours with a fire response about an hour after we left."

George didn't look that surprised and the wheels in his mind were still turning around running like a finely-tuned Aston Martin.

"Loose ends," George said.

"Or something spooked them," Bob replied. "What's our next move on this George?"

"It is obvious they don't mind killing, so this is something just you and I need to sort until we can blow the whole thing open."

"I think I'm going to get Sally down to our daughter's for a couple of weeks."

"Probably a good idea," George agreed. "Bob, I want you to find out as much as you can about this unit in Hounslow. I'll dig up what I can on the company itself called 'Scientia Global' but remember, someone could be watching you."

Bob had been through enough trauma and pressure in his career to take things for granted. Occasionally, he did feel the strain, but he also knew how to channel his energy and right now he knew he wanted another pint.

25

Things had worked smoothly so far, and Kyle Greenwood had fulfilled his major tasks without any hitches. Now his primary role was to monitor Donald Lewis and keep him on the right path until the job was completed. But that afternoon, following the conclusion of a debate on the financial rewards being heaped on the directors of the energy companies, Kyle was concerned about his duty's ramblings to the Shadow Cabinet's Secretary of State for International Trade in the Strangers Bar. It wasn't so much that the information could be described as 'the infatuations of a man out of his depth and living in a fantasy world', what was concerning to Kyle was that the Labour member seemed to be taking it in, not just letting him waffle like a droning noise past his ears.

"Things will change soon, Nick, mark my words."

"How so, Donald? Is this a party plan or your own endeavours and ideas?"

"It's time as a nation we reaped the benefits that were sown hundreds of years ago; we established the finest empire and financial institutions and we have allowed others to exploit us and keep us down."

Lewis sipped some more brandy and was suddenly acutely aware that he had probably said too much to the opposition.

"What I mean is, we need to look at ourselves, our financial standing and become great again."

"You're talking about stepping away from a world banking system which is balanced and controlled, to be driven by some sort of narcissistic leader?"

Kyle walked over to the side of Donald Lewis.

"Excuse me, Sir," he said to Lewis then looked at the Labour

Member of Parliament. "Apologies, Sir, but I have been asked to bring a matter to Mr Lewis's attention from his constituency that needs an immediate response."

The shadow cabinet minister nodded and stood up, picking up his glass of apple and mango juice and as he left said,

"Interesting subject, Donald, we will have to catch up again soon."

The look on the MP's face was a mixture of rebuff and embarrassment as if he had been scolded by the head boy at his boarding school.

"What is the problem, Kyle?" Lewis spoke with a measure of authority and stuttering as if trying to regain his grip on the situation.

"Minister, I have to remind you that the long-term success of our project requires stealth and secrecy without drawing any attention to you other than your normal ministerial duties."

Kyle responded with a soft tone trying to portray the situation as a slight slip-up, but deep down he was worried that the MP was becoming a bit of a liability.

"I have done as requested, Kyle, for your masters. I have allowed you to be in my entourage and given you access to key people and information because you have provided me with leverage and a promise of great things and of course with a financial bonus, but I haven't seen much recently."

Donald Lewis had spoken the last line almost in a whisper.

"I am just a small link in this project, Minister," Kyle responded, glancing around the bar ensuring others weren't taking a keen interest in them, "If you require more, you should ask me so I can take this back to the appropriate people, he added.

Donald Lewis downed the last of his brandy and stood looking around briefly before his gaze returned to Kyle Greenwood and he spoke quietly,

"How much longer do we need to play this game before I-" he made a noise to clear his throat, acutely aware he had said something wrong, "Before 'we' can reap the benefits?"

"I am not privy to all the facts, Sir, but I will see what I can find out."

Donald Lewis left the bar and headed off for a well-deserved snooze in the next debate and Kyle Greenwood thought it was time to share his concerns with his masters.

He made his way back to the small office at the eastern wing and retrieved the mobile from the desk and sent a quick small text message to 'Kr', 'ADVICE NEEDED REGARDING MISFIRING MINI PETROL ENGINE.' He switched the phone off knowing the response would be a few hours away but instead of putting it back into the desk, he took his empty backpack from the hat stand and started putting all of his personal papers and kit into it.

26

Most of the cameras were fixed in place around the building, covering a view from each corner to corner but this security camera was on a pole in the middle of the car parking area; it moved slowly and locked onto a dark green shabby-looking Ford Fiesta as it ground to a halt about half a metre away from the thick fencing surrounding the industrial unit. The car was barely illuminated by a few of the units' outside lights in the darkness of the evening, but enough to see that it was dented and scratched all over with enough damage to almost look like it had just finished a stock car rally.

The security guard monitoring the screen couldn't believe what he saw next as a single person all in black and a hoodie got out of the car with what looked like a wine bottle with a piece of rag stuffed in the top, lit it and fired a Molotov cocktail into the car and then ran off into the scrub, disappearing almost instantly. The guard immediately called the fire service and then his boss to explain what was going on.

The nearest fire stations were Feltham and Twickenham, but these were currently unavailable, so a single appliance was sent from Heston which arrived after about nine minutes and was greeted by a fully-developed car on fire. The officer in charge got his crew to work with two hose reels and then made his way towards the unit's main gate. He pressed the intercom button and was instantly met with the voice of the security guard.

"What can I do for you chief?"

"Can I have access to the unit to check there is no fire spread or damage inside your compound?"

"That won't be possible."

"I need to ensure the fire is not spreading from the fence or heat is affecting the main building."

"I will detail our security to check it for you."

"You do know that in a fire situation I can demand access into this building and compound and by law, you have to let me in?"

The security guard was on his phone with his boss as this request was being stressed.

"If you can wait a minute, I will check and get back to you."

The frustration was building in the experienced watch manager as he waited for two, three then four minutes. Just as he was about to press the intercom button again, one of his crew members called him up on his fireground radio.

"Boss, you had better come back; a message has just come over the radio that access is not required."

"Where has it come from?"

"Area Manager Sykes has just contacted control and ordered it. He said he will deal with it personally."

"I hope he takes full responsibility if the building is damaged then because I ain't taking any shit from this."

As he walked back to the scene of the fire which was just a burnt-out shell now with a single hose reel being used to dampen it down, he wondered if it was worth contacting the police to investigate the obvious doubtful origin and check to see if the car was stolen, or just give it all to Sykes.

Just as he was going to request a police attendance, an unmarked car with blue lights came crawling up and stopped about twenty yards from them. The driver stayed in his seat, but another guy got out and walked up to talk to him.

"That's quick, I was just going to call for you chaps."

"We were in the area and saw the lights and thought we would check it out. As we drove down, we called it in for us to deal with if required."

"Right-o fella, we are about done; I just need a few details of the vehicle and a VIN if I can get one and we will be out of your way. Oh, and best of luck getting into that place if you want to look at the CCTV."

The fire crew collected all their equipment and drove about a hundred yards down the road to make use of a fire hydrant to fill their tank back up.

Lenny Andrews stood by the burnt-out shell of the car showing no interest but glancing occasionally at the fire crew until they drove away. He got back into the car, and they moved to the main gate which opened as they pulled up to it. Both went into the security office and viewed the CCTV footage, and both agreed there was nothing that could help them or identify anyone and so they assumed it was another stolen car just being dumped and torched like so many others would be all around the country tonight. What they didn't see was that from the moment the car was set alight, the hooded man in black had slowly moved around in the darkness and the fringes of the industrial estate to watch the whole show from start to finish with great interest.

27

Emerson had seen the footage of the car fire and had never really been that bothered, following the explanation given by Georgina Williams' men and the information received from Sykes. Danny Van Bloche, however, wasn't as comfortable.

"Sir, with respect I think we may need to look at a few things here; this has come at a time when recent developments have occurred."

"What do you mean developments?"

"Greenwood has raised some concerns over Donald Lewis's gossip with other people in the corridors of power, the need to deal with that cleaning company and now this car fire right outside." Van Bloche's tone showed no emotion just a delivery of detail and information.

"We are very close to the end game, Danny; the trial of the program Kimmy has developed will be tested this evening and if successful, we are only a few days away from completion."

"May I have your permission to investigate the Lewis concern, Sir?"

"Yes, but at a distance and if you feel action is required, report back to me and I will resolve the problem in my own special way."

"Very good, Sir," Van Bloche turned and as he left Emerson again asked him to send Kimmy in.

"Having gone through the process and reading your report, everything looks plausible."

Kimmy nodded.

"And you're fairly sure if this Ezra Gateway does detect anything, it won't make its way back to here?"

"I am confident at this point as long as I don't attempt to move any financial blocks, the system won't know we are there and if it does, I will sever the link long before it tracks back to us." Kimmy never faltered or showed a nervous worry in his reply.

"But how will the program function when we use it against the Cerberus Lock and Jorogumo before we start moving funds?"

"Ultimately, it will be impossible not to notice the missing funds when downloaded but my program will leave a copy and snapshot of what is there for a set time period and as the time runs down, a series of spike programs will send any traceable routes around hundreds of other servers until the clock completes its countdown and we will have vanished."

"You're starting the trial run on Ezra at 23:00 tonight." It was a confirmation not a question from Emerson.

"Yes, Sir, I anticipate about five to seven hours the program will have to run as it ghosts through the system."

"And how will you know you have got right in?"

"I am expecting a file path to lead us to a screen with one of the files, titled Deus Aurum which on opening will give us access to bank accounts and funds, but I won't enable the drain-down part of the program, I will retrace the ghosting process and ensure all doors are closed behind, then at least this way there shouldn't be any trace of anyone accessing the system."

"Good, I will join you here this evening at 22:00."

Kimmy nodded and left the office closing the door behind him. Emerson turned his swivel chair around and closed his eyes, thinking through the conversation he'd previously had with Danny.

28

That Wednesday morning the routine was normal as Jane brought in Bob's cup of tea and overnight reports. She placed the files on his desk and put his tea down and was turning to leave when Bob asked for the southwest building consultation register for the last three years. Jane returned a few minutes later with two files, one marked Local Authority Building Control and the other Approved Inspector Building Control. Both files had a start date of 2018 with no end date which would be added at the end of five years to be filed as a period log.

Bob wasn't sure if the consultation would have been done with a local authority, but this was the smaller file, so he decided to work through this one first. The register only had a date, the name of the consulting officer, and the name of the building with a postcode and reference; the actual consultation would be either on the service's computer system or if older, in filed documents held in storage.

It took Bob two more cups of tea before he finished with the local authority register and then he started on the approved inspectors. He eventually came across the file reference which as it turned out was a good result for him. The approved inspectors used were a local firm based in London and a place he had often visited to carry out consultations face-to-face with one specific inspector. He took a sticky note and scribbled down their reference and grabbing his jacket as he left, he passed the files back to Jane.

"Just popping out to lunch Janey, you can file these away again, thanks."

A few streets off Oxford Street the offices of Hephaestus Approved Inspectors were located over the fourth and fifth floors of a seven-storey building. Bob walked the stairs to their reception and was about to open his mouth when he heard,

"Bob, you old scoundrel you must have heard the kettle was on!"

Bob turned as a slim-built man with neatly trimmed grey hair walked towards him smiling broadly and holding out his hand.

"Johhny boy, good to see you and yes, get that tea on the go."

They shook hands and patted each other's shoulders. John Lutin had been in the building game since he was a boy, literally. Initially trained as a surveyor on sites, he had learned his trade well and progressed up to a building inspector with the local authority before being head-hunted by Hephaestus where he dealt with all their big projects. John didn't need to ask how Bob liked his tea; he knew from all their time working together over the years on many consultations and projects.

They sat down in his plush office in a couple of comfy chairs with a small round table and a view of the London skyline.

"What brings you down, Bob? I thought you had passed the mantle of this stuff over a while back."

"I need some help, John, with a consultation that was completed a couple of years ago and was wondering if you could let me look at any details you still hold?"

"Have you the reference?"

Bob passed the sticky note over to John *'HOUNS / IND347 / CAT1 / 04-03-2019'*

"It's a CAT1 unit which may have restricted access which I have; anything specific?"

"Ideally, some background detail of its designated use and plans would be good."

"Ok, I can have a look to see what we still hold, but you won't be able to copy anything, only make notes."

"That's fine, I've got a pad with me," Bob replied.

John put his cup down and left the office returning a few minutes later with a cardboard tube and an A4 file.

"It's a strange one, Bob. We initially did the consultation with fire, and everything was completed as per spec."

"But?" Bob said looking at his friend inquisitively.

"Well according to the client information, the building was taken over by a company based in Bahrain and then the internal layout was completely altered a few months after original completion and signed off at the time by Neil Collins, one of our inspectors."

"What am I missing, Johnny?"

"That was the last job Neil completed for us. We received notification that he had sold up and left the country a day or so later."

"Ordinarily, I would say that's odd but these days it's possible," said Bob.

"The job was all paid for on time and everything filed as complete," John added.

Bob took the A4 file and opened it to read the building design report which stated 'an industrial unit consisting of four floors with a basement and lower basement indicated as a plant and services level.' The use had been described as 'light industrial with high levels of information technology', which would have meant lots of computers or computer-aided machines like 3D printers or processing machines. Bob put the file down and opened the tube of plans which consisted of six A3 sheets in colour. One sheet gave all the elevations in scale, four sheets for each level from the ground to the third floor and the last sheet of the basements.

"I'll just go and make us a fresh cup, Bob, take your time." John left the office and Bob knew he would be a good ten minutes.

The floor plans looked as normal as any other industrial unit with stairwells at either end of the building, the lift shaft was specified at 120-minute fire separation which must have been requested by the client. It was when Bob came to the basement plans that had him scratching his head. At first look, it seemed that both levels were the same layout with a protected stair serving both up to the ground level, but on closer examination, Bob saw a marking on the plan mirrored on both basement outlines.

"It's not two, it's one basement," he mumbled to himself and followed up slightly louder with, "a bloody big basement at that."

He put the plans down, took out his pad and started making some notes, scribbling the measurements and a rough plan of the building layout. He rolled up the plans and put them back into the tube just as John came back in with two fresh cups of tea.

They spent another thirty minutes catching up on football, namely John's Toffees and their struggle to get away from the relegation zone. Then they shook hands and said their goodbyes with a promise to go out for a curry soon.

29

It wasn't unusual for Georgina Williams to be summoned to Thomas Fawling, in the Deputy Commissioner's office for briefings, reports or the occasional friendly coffee and a chat, but she didn't expect an official email which included copies to the Commissioner and Assistant Commissioner. Perhaps one of them was retiring and she was being viewed as a possible replacement, she thought. The email only stated she was to attend the meeting at 11:30 Thursday morning in full dress uniform; no other details were given.

On entering the Deputy Commissioner PA's office, she was told to go into Briefing Room two and as soon as she opened the door, a small shudder went down her spine, though she made sure she showed no external signs to the people in the room. It was set up as if for a job interview, with the Deputy Commissioner sitting behind the desk, looking across at a single chair. The worry for Georgina Williams was caused by the other two people flanking him.

One was Commander Jimmy 'Jock' Johnston, probably the Met's most respected and feared person to get on the wrong side of. He had served in most of the specialist units of the Met at some point but had come to fame in Protection Command after taking a blade to the stomach when an Iranian asylum seeker on release had attempted to attack the Prime Minister during a tour of the newly-refurbished Ash Grove Bus Depot. Jock wasn't wearing a stab vest as he was walking alongside the PM at the time of the attack and the outer cordon protection teams had missed the man who had hidden on a new Wright SRM double-decker. It wasn't so much what happened that had added to his legendary status, it was as the Iranian screamed in his face, Jock with a four-inch blade in his stomach just looked at him then head-butted the guy, knocking him clean out, then turned to the

PM and asked to be excused as the security teams closed around securing the area. Rumours obviously had been exaggerated that as he head-butted the guy, he had said 'see you pal' but this was pure fantasy.

Georgina had never worked with him but knew all about him, that he was now heading up the Aviation Policing Command, looking after Heathrow and London City Airports.

It was the other person sitting at the table who raised the most concern, Director General Heather Smallwood of the Independent Office for Police Conduct or IOPC. Heather had worked in local authority all her career from local and borough councils and was now the driving force for the Home Office. In simple terms, they policed the police which included the ability to initiate their own investigations, from police firearms incidents, rumours, Intel or crimes committed by officers.

"Before we start, Miss Williams, I must inform you that this meeting is informal but will be recorded with minutes taken. You are welcome to leave at any time and you can request legal representation to be present if you wish."

Deputy Commissioner Fawling spoke with a quiet tone of confidence and Williams knew at that moment she was going nowhere, to leave or ask for legal representation was like saying, 'ok you've got me, I'm busted'. Georgina Williams hadn't gotten to where she was without fighting all the way and she wasn't about to break now.

"No, Sir, I am fine with everything stated," she said confidently.

They were the only ones in the room, but the meeting was being recorded externally and notes were taken by other IOPC personnel. Thomas looked at Heather Smallwood and nodded.

The mood relaxed a little as Heather Smallwood began the meeting and used first names as a way of keeping things informal at this time.

"Georgina, you are aware of officers Andrews and Daniels

based out of Lavender Hill?"

"Yes, Ma-am." It would be stupid to reply with no.

"And you have detailed these officers in the past with tasks or requests?"

"Yes, Ma-am, I have on occasion used these officers if they were available."

"Can I ask why these officers are used by you more than others?"

The one thing Williams was good at was creating a story instantly and being able to spin it with variable directions under pressure.

"Often Intel or operational requirements have come to me in and around the Fulham, Wandsworth and Brixton areas and they have been successful in resolving or reporting the Intel needed to act upon."

"Do you use these officers elsewhere, either within the London area or outside?"

At this point, she knew that with Jock Johnston in the room she may have a little room to manoeuvre.

"On occasion, Ma-am, I have asked them to investigate or gather Intel north of the river in and around Shepherds Bush or Kensington."

"Why didn't you use the other local stations to carry out this work?"

"Ma-am, some of the foreign gangs in recent months have evaded us during some of our sting operations and my initial concern was information was being leaked and therefore I wanted two officers that have, in recent months, proved useful to do some monitoring duties."

"And have they been successful?"

"They have found evidence of previous activities but nothing current."

Fawling had been made aware of the Albanian problems some weeks ago and this had been given to him by Georgina Williams, so there was some truth in the statement.

"And as far as you are aware, these officers have not been involved in any way with other foreign gangs or individuals?"

"No, Ma-am, I am not."

Heather sat back in her chair, as Jock Johnston cleared his throat and passed some papers over the desk.

"These images are of Daniels and Anderson talking to one Yuseff Hamed Hamin, an ex-Moroccan national who works out of Heathrow's cargo terminal."

She looked and knew it would be pointless to say it wasn't them.

"Yes, that's them," she replied.

"We have been increasing surveillance in and around the cargo terminal recently, based on a tip from a source in Turkey's Ministry of Internal Affairs over the smuggling of tobacco in and out of the country."

Georgina Williams looked again at the photos in front of her, more to hide the rising rage inside her.

"I am unaware of their normal duties or investigations but if you require any extra resources from me or my department?" She already knew the answer but was determined to paint the right picture.

"That won't be necessary, there is an operation already in place."

Heather Smallwood sat forward again and gathered her paperwork together, with a steely-eyed look at Williams. She stood up and spoke softly,

"As well as the operation that is in place, a full internal investigation has begun and therefore you may need to assist us further. So, I suggest you keep your diary free unless required only by the Commissioner himself."

"Yes, Ma-am, of course."

Georgina stayed in her seat and after Heather Smallwood left the room, Thomas Fawling said,

"You can go now, Georgina, but if anything is found linking you to this muddy business, I will personally nail you to the wall."

She stood and nodded to both officers and left the room, at the back of her mind wanting to tear the throats out of the two incompetent officers that could have wrecked everything.

30

Emerson took up a seat next to Kimmy at 09:50 and looked at his watch and the screen which was blank apart from a prompt cursor in the top left corner. Kimmy sat with a notepad open in front of him with a page full of scribbled text and symbols and an external 16 terra byte hard drive ready to plug in. There was no starting early and Emerson was aware that the whole process had to be handled and run by Kimmy, with no intervention unless it became obvious to him that they had been caught red-handed during the process, which he felt the Korean genius would probably have already set up any countermeasures in his program if that occurred.

At 09:59, Kimmy plugged his external drive in and began to work his way along servers scattered around the world; it would take an hour of links, jumps and hoops before the program trial would commence. He weaved his path through a couple of secondary schools in America, a laundry company's booking system in Australia, and a Japanese firework company and continued to worm a link all the way to Italy. Emerson admired the plan that back-flowing the link on detection would be following a time zone countdown which would add more time to cut any connection back to them if detected. The last link Kimmy had put in was a church website which he knew would also look normal as he finally accessed the Vatican's server systems.

At dead on 23:00, he entered the start-up code for his ghosting program and watched for the next 30 minutes as the program jumped through the links to its destination point; when it arrived at the required point, Kimmy entered another code and sat back but kept his eyes fixed on the screen.

"The first few minutes will be key to this working, Sir."

Emerson just sat for another twenty minutes watching the screen then retreated to his office. He sat back in his chair and took out four mobiles from the drawer and switched them on. There were no messages on any of the phones which meant no problems and he switched them off and replaced them in the drawer. He took out his private mobile and messaged Danny Van Bloche: 'TRIAL RUN IN PROGRESS, MY OFFICE TOMORROW 10:00'. He rose from the seat, walked across to his coffee machine and poured himself a drink; he knew it was going to be a long evening.

For four hours, Kimmy had watched the screen like an eagle with no red flags shown or walls being put up, but just as he glanced down to put his hand on the packet of extra strong mints, he had to help his concentration, the screen flickered just briefly which went unnoticed by him. At just after 02:30, Kimmy put his hand up and looked towards Emerson in his office. He came out and sat by his side and noticed the files scrolling down the screen.

"I thought you said it would take five to seven hours, Kimmy?"

"There has been no change during the program, so I would assume it cleared the Ezra Gateway which meant there were fewer doors to go through."

Kimmy took his pencil and pointed on the screen to the bottom right where the file Deus Aurum was located.

"Well done. Now, Kimmy, how do you get out without raising any flags?"

"In the same way as getting in, Sir, retrace but ghosting, any attempt to just pull the plug would just be like putting a target above our heads."

"Let me know when you've cleared back without any issues."

"Yes, Sir."

Emerson went back to his office and three hours later, Kimmy disconnected the external drive and nodded to Emerson who waved his hand to call him in.

"Again, well done Kimmy, get yourself away now have a rest, back in about 10ish tomorrow so we can review everything and plan the next step."

Kimmy nodded and left while Emerson sat back with his thoughts, looking forward to finishing his plan and reaping the huge benefits with absolutely nobody knowing who was responsible.

31

George Calian watched from a safe distance as a dark blue Mercedes SUV drove up to the gate of Scientia Global; the security must have known who it was because there was no buzzing on the intercom. George briefly recalled back to late the night before, when he'd had a great time setting the hidden camera. He'd aimed it towards the gate from the adjoining unit's roof, using a wheelie bin and a couple of wooden pallets he'd found at the back of the building. Now, he watched and operated the camera remotely to capture people and vehicles going in and out, as he sat in his car hidden away at another part of the industrial estate but in a position to see the road up to the gate. It was odd, he thought, considering the size of the unit, how not many people had entered the site; from about 07:30 to 09:00 he had counted only 12 so far. From their attire, they appeared a mix of young adults with a couple of older ladies, possibly cleaners or canteen workers if they had one. All the staff had to buzz in and show their I.Ds to the camera at the main gate which is why he was interested in this specific vehicle. Although he couldn't see their faces clearly, he took some pictures and made sure he captured the registration plate and worked out that there was a man and a woman in the car.

He looked at his watch and decided he had better pop into the office to show his face for an hour, check his emails and put some reports together which would keep his bosses happy and show he was doing his normal work duties. Just as he was about to drive off, he noticed someone in a smart suit with a canvas shoulder bag walking in the direction of the unit. From a distance, he appeared to George as if he could be Japanese or Chinese, but it was difficult to make him out fully. He decided to switch the camera on again and took some more pictures then headed off to Holburn.

On entering his office, he switched on his office laptop without sitting down then headed to make a coffee and stood for a few minutes sipping his drink glancing around the office just to check for normality. Nothing seemed different so he returned and sat down. Over the next hour or so he cleared emails, finished some outstanding reports and checked that he wasn't required to pick up anyone else's work because of sickness or leave. At 12:37 he switched off his laptop and as he left, shouted across the office to Jean Tully the administrator, more for the whole office to hear, that he was grabbing some lunch and going to check on a couple of things. Jean knew him well and his routines which meant she may not see him for a couple of days, but she also knew that if needed, she could get him on his mobile if not straight away usually within an hour or two at most.

George switched his mobile off, took out the SIM card and headed back to Hounslow, parked in the same place as earlier and took a small gun sight out and noticed the SUV was still parked. He got comfortable, opened a pack of Jammy Dodgers and waited.

32

"And this has been confirmed I presume?" Emerson's initial demeanour had soured very quickly.

"I'm afraid so, Sir. Williams contacted me through the secure system, and I managed to arrange a meeting without any prying eyes or ears." Danielle Keller was standing almost to attention as if speaking to her Headmaster.

"Is there any way back to us?"

"I don't think they can make a direct link between us and the Met through her, but I certainly feel that her stooges could sale her down the river if they are put in front of a firing squad and I honestly don't know how things would play out."

Emerson looked at Van Bloche. "Danny, what are your thoughts on this?"

"If this was back home, all the problems could be cleaned, people paid off and within a week or two things would be back to normal."

"I sense a 'but' coming."

"Sir, we can't just make these two idiots of hers disappear, there would be too many questions, but we also can't risk Georgina being investigated further."

"I am assuming you have something in mind?"

"There is a possible solution that should work, at least until we have completed our goal and disappeared."

Emerson sat back in his chair feeling a little more relaxed, his security chief had never let him down and he knew he would have planned weeks in advance for possible unexpected turns or twists, long before he knew his master would ask him.

"We get Georgina Williams out of the country immediately with a small pay-off and hide her off-grid in a nice place with a promise of her full cut on completion of the operation."

"Do you have somewhere in mind?"

"The Inagua Islands, Sir."

"Never heard of them."

"They are part of the Bahamas, but further down off the tip of Cuba."

Danny went on to explain how he would transport her out of London on a container ship and in the Caribbean organise a transfer to a waiting motor cruiser. From there, she would be given some fake identification and a reasonable house had already been rented in Matthew Town. The new identity was to include her as an author to back up the plan of being reclusive in her work.

"How soon can you get this in action, Danny?"

"Shanghai Shipping has a container ship due to leave on the morning tide, tomorrow."

"Danielle, is Williams aware of this plan?"

"Yes, Sir, Danny had briefed me on the options before my meeting and after going through it, with the initial suggested fee and what her final pay-off from the operation was going to be, she agreed."

"Do you foresee any complications?"

"No, Sir, she has already cut herself off from her two idiot stooges and we will pay her an initial one million US dollars into her new identity's account and as already mentioned, we have rented a basic furnished home including some transportation available to her."

"Ok, put it into action but Danielle, I want you to deliver her to the island just in case she changes her mind and decides to go in another direction."

Van Bloche and Keeler left the office and Emerson, although feeling troubled, was confident that following the successful trial the other night that they could complete everything and be in the clear long before detection or discovery. As he watched one of the monitors in his office, as his security team drove through the gate, he felt confident they were nearly at the endpoint. He had no idea that a couple of hundred yards away, a camera was clicking furiously.

33

Bob was keen to sit down with George and show him the plans he had reproduced and update him on the information he had found out. However, he also knew that sitting in a pub, even in the garden, with A3 plans and a Detective Inspector of the Met could look a bit out of the ordinary. He popped into the Lord Nelson at lunchtime and asked if the barman could pass this letter on to George later when he got in. He walked through to the garden and left via the back way.

He decided to visit a couple of stations to catch up with some of the FIT teams just to pass the time and ensure that he was seen out and about. He had also decided to visit Islington Station and have a chat with their FIT team about the flat fire in Catherall Road. As always, on entering an LFB station he was made to feel welcome, and the kettle was put on straight away.

He was sitting at the mess table with Jerome Afamefuna, one of the FIT teams' Watch Managers when the Borough Commander came into the room with an empty cup in his hand.

"Hi, Bob, how are things?"

Bob stood up and shook hands with Giles Young.

"Hey, Toastie, I'm good. How are you getting on with your new position here?"

Jerome wasn't expecting the relaxed manner in which the two men spoke and had never heard anyone call the Commander by his nickname to his face. So, to escape the moment, he stood and said, "Tea, boss?" to which Giles handed him his cup. As he went to make another cup of tea, Bob and Giles sat down.

Both men had worked in their younger days across the capital on large fires when mobilised during make-ups or reliefs and Giles had acquired the nickname 'Toastie' because whenever he went into jobs in breathing apparatus, he always seemed to get so close to the fires and was often informed that his fire kit was smoking, just before he would say 'getting a bit toastie in here'. Jerome sat back down and listened to both men chatting for ten minutes before Giles stood and said,

"Good to see you, fella, always welcome here for a brew, if you're in the area," and walked back to his office.

"Known him a while then, Guv?" Jerome said more of a statement.

"We bumped into each other on big stuff or as reliefs mainly, although he did the occasional out duty with us at Abbott Road."

"They say he was a good guy to have when the shit hit the fan?" This time Jerome was fishing for information.

"I was with him a couple of times in some pretty scary moments; one was the Beckton Treatment works when a large storage building went up in the small hours with a couple of security guys missing."

"We did that as a case study at training school," Jerome responded.

"Well, the place was rammed with all sorts of nasty chemicals, and we managed to find the security guys in a bad way near some sodium hydroxide tanks which were becoming involved." Bob paused for a sip of tea then continued, "We dragged both guys out who were still alive, just, but in a bad way found near to some other pH neutralisers that were already becoming involved in the fire and they were beginning to gas off." Bob took another sip of tea and looked over his shoulder to make sure Giles wasn't standing there. "Giles put himself in front of me as a shield and took all the punishment with a 45 hose on spray, while I dragged both casualties clear enough before the storage tanks failed, which would have been like pouring salt on a slug for those guys."

Bob finished his story and asked for another cup of tea and carefully planned his next direction of the conversation. Jerome having made two fresh cups, sat back down and Bob started asking how things were in the FIT team; did they need any more equipment? Was there any additional training that would be of benefit? Just general questions which he had put to the other two teams he had visited earlier. He made some notes on a pad and as he finished writing the things Jerome had raised and requested, he said,

"And the OICs of the FIT teams are following procedural paths?"

Jerome made a slight shift and cleared his throat. "Well, Guv, generally our normal OICs follow all protocols as laid down and refer to specialist guide notes, if required, or contact you or the FI Duty Officer as a last resort."

Bob nodded understanding and as Jerome hadn't felt the urge to continue, he added, "Don't worry, this is just between you and me."

"Well, a couple of weeks ago, we started the shift with a replacement SO, some guy Drayton, who said he was part of a research team looking at improving the efficiency of fire investigation and simplifying it to achieve better results." It was Jerome's turn to sip his tea and look at the door then continue, "Well, we had a fatal flat fire in a block, up near Goats Park, which had the usual attendance, but this Drayton guy goes in with two police officers for about twenty minutes then comes back with a signed bit of paper saying now handed over to police."

"Did you question the procedure with him?"

"Scooby Watson, who was our assigned fire dog handler that night, did mention it but was shot down with the threat of Area Manager Sykes putting him on the river station."

Bob had the confirmation he wanted, so he took the next moments to play it down a little by suggesting if there was a piece of paper stating the police had taken control, then as far as they were concerned, that was the end of the matter but promised to take it up with senior management to ensure existing procedures were to be followed, or that an update was put out to all FIT teams. He stood and took a ten-pound note out of his wallet, giving it to Jerome to put in the tea boat and thanked him before tapping the door window on Giles Young's office and waving goodbye.

34

The next day just after 11:00, Bob parked his car at Euston Fire Station and informed the Watch Officer that he would be back in about an hour. Then he walked up the road to a Pret-a-Manager to pick up a couple of coffees before heading towards Midland Street. About a hundred metres down on the left was the staff and contractors' entrance to the British Library. Bob spoke to a security officer via an intercom and a couple of minutes later, a woman smartly dressed in a suit opened the door for him. He put the coffee and his backpack down and gave the lady a big hug.

"Mrs Bryers, you look great!"

Steve Bryers' wife hugged him just as tightly.

"Thanks, Bob, the other gent you asked access for is already here."

Bob picked his backpack and coffees up and followed Sarah Bryers down the stairs into the basement area, to an empty restoration room that was used for the repairs and cleaning of many of the books and other artefacts such as papers, manuscripts, maps and even sound recordings. Bob thanked her and she told him to ping her a text when they were done.

"This is a nice arrangement you have, Bob," said George as Bob entered the room and closed the door.

"Apart from the fact that the wife of my best mate is the Head of Corporate Assurance, I have done quite a few fire-safety favours for the library and some of the governing board members here."

George joined Bob at one of the angled restoration tables where he rolled out the drawings of the unit he had sketched from his notes and began to explain the layout and the strange design of the basement. When he finished, George took some freshly printed photographs out and placed them over the plans of the unit from the outside.

"Scientia or Science Global is recognised worldwide for cyber security and is owned and run by this man." George put another picture down which had been cut from a magazine, "Emerson Jacobs was born in Zimbabwe to a wealthy farming family; they had to leave in a hurry during the troubles and set up in South Africa."

Bob looked at the picture. "He doesn't look like a farmer."

George explained that as a child he had been sent to a boarding school in England and then to university, as well as studying Software Engineering, including Cyber Security, he studied Business and Marketing.

"After finishing university, it gets a little grey; there are some vague details of working for a couple of companies in California on internet systems but then nothing until about seven years ago when Scientia popped up."

"In South Africa?" Bob asked.

"No, strangely the first registered place was Manama in Bahrain."

"I'm no expert, George, but that seems a bit of a strange place to start."

"Chances are it was where the finances were raised."

George then put a folded copy of the Financial Times down with a pen-ringed circle on an article which read *'Scientia Climbing High'* the ringed area stated the company had a current value of twelve million pounds sterling and was focused on building up to compete with the best.

"I managed to get some information from a couple of internet sources I know, that let's just say operate on the other side of the firewalls and they both stated that this company has some serious muscle. Anyway, one of the guys said he knew that the company puts out challenges for whiz-kids to solve and if they do, they get invited in for another test and could earn ten grand a month if good enough."

"And did one of your contacts get invited?"

"Yes, he got invited but out of the four in the room, he came second and was hammered by a young guy he thought was Russian who claimed the prize and was taken upstairs almost straight away to meet the boss. Meanwhile, they were politely shown the door with a 'better luck next time' pat on the back and a Costa Coffee free drink voucher."

George then placed some pictures of a dark blue Mercedes SUV leaving the gate at the unit, including a zoomed-in copy of the two people in the car.

"These two, though, are what is worrying me."

Bob looked at them and didn't recognise them from the images and couldn't place them anywhere in his recent movements or dealings.

"I haven't come across them with anyone I've been in contact with over the last couple of weeks," he said.

"The information on them is sketchy at best, but I did manage to find out that they both served in the military in South Africa, which probably means if they are employed by Scientia now, they were likely to have been above just run-of-the-mill squaddies which potentially makes them very dangerous." George's tone was level but there was most definitely a hint of concern showing on his face.

George moved the photographs to the side and looked again at the plans and took some more images of the unit out of his own backpack. There were some photographs of the unit from various angles and a couple of Google Earth aerial views showing the complete perimeter.

"I think, Bob, we need to get in there and see exactly what is going on."

"If you can get us past the external security undetected, I am sure with these plans there's bound to be some way in, like a service hatch, storeroom or access shaft into the basement which could give us entry with the help of a few tools."

George nodded and started to clear up his photos and images as Bob rolled the plans up.

"The best time would be early hours on a Sunday morning from around 1-ish but before 3 am because of daylight breaking and also it seems there is only a single security guard in a control room until 8 in the morning."

"Ok, George, what do you need from me in the meantime?"

George handed him all the images and photos, except the images of the people and said, "See if you can locate our way in and I'm going to talk to some of my contacts to see if I can find out any more on these South Africans; who they may be or are linked to."

Bob took his personal mobile out and sent a text message to Sarah Bryers who knocked on the door two minutes later. She escorted them back to the door that exited onto Midland Road and gave Bob another hug, then pressed the green button to release the door lock. George went first, turning left and Bob a couple of seconds later, turning right. They had agreed to meet the next evening in the Nelson.

35

Danielle drove the SUV around the block three times and after each lap, there didn't appear to be anything out of the ordinary. She still wasn't happy with having to babysit Georgina Williams for the next fourteen days or so but although Danny wasn't expecting the request from their employer, he had assured her that a plane ticket would have her back to the Bahamas and on the next flight back to London as soon as she dropped Williams off at her new residence.

The MV Doumu was due to ship out of the Tilbury Container Port at 07:12 and Danielle had to make sure the timing of everything went like clockwork. The first stage had already been completed with a couple of suitcases picked up the night before from the foyer of Williams' apartment block which overlooked St Katherine's Docks. Now at just after five in the morning, she saw Georgina Williams exit her apartment block dressed in Lycra leggings, white trainers, a headband and iPod buds in her ears as if about to go for an early morning jog or walk; there was no music though, just directions and orders to be given by Danielle as she set off.

She started walking at a brisk pace up Thomas More Street, turned right onto East Smithfield, crossed over and headed up John Fisher Street. Danielle drove behind steadily, before passing her and turning right into Royal Mint Street, then looping around Dock Street to check that there was nobody following. As Williams passed the 'Jack the Ripper Museum' on Cable Street, she heard the command in her headphones,

"Go left at Back Church Lane under the bridge then right into Pinchin Lane. Wait under the trees about a hundred yards down on the left."

Danielle drove another loop and pulled up under the tree in Pinchin Lane, leant across the seats and opened the door.

Williams got in and Danielle set off for the forty-minute drive to Tilbury. The first couple of miles, she drove at a slow, steady speed, constantly checking her rear-view mirror. On reaching the A13, she sped up a little and then headed into Grays where she made a couple of final loops around Grays Town Park before pulling into Grays Railway Station car park alongside a parked blue transit van, with Fulham Freight written on two magnetic stickers attached to both sides. Danielle got out first, took another set of keys from her pocket and clicked the van open. She looked in the back of the van which was half-filled with boxes and crates; two boxes at the back labelled 'marine engine components' which in fact, held Georgina Williams' suitcases. She walked back to the car and gave Williams a bright orange tabard which also had 'Fulham Freight' printed on the back.

"Put this on and when we get near to the gate, put your hard hat on as well."

As Williams got in the van's passenger seat, Danielle made sure there was nothing left in the car and checked that it was locked before jumping into the van. It was only a short drive to the main dock gate and after checking on his manifest sheet, the security guard raised the barrier expecting this van to be back very soon with only a couple of boxes to be dropped off. At the dockside, both Keeler and Williams got out and carried a box each up the gangplank and into the MV Doumo.

Just inside the superstructure, two men dressed in the same orange hi-vis jackets and yellow hard hats came the other way. Keeler passed one of them the SUV keys and they walked down the gangplank and drove off in the van. The security guard saw the van coming back with two people in and raised the barrier for them to exit, waving them through without even looking up from his copy of 'The Racing Post' and checking the favourite in the 3:30 at Ascot.

Back on the MV Doumo, as the mooring lines were being released, Keeler and Williams were shown to the cabin which they would occupy for the next couple of weeks, depending on the weather. The room was cramped, with a double bunk but at least it had a small shower room and a toilet, giving them some sense of privacy from the crew. The crewman that showed them to their cabin identified himself simply as Chang and said that they were to stay inside the cabin for the next six hours until the ship was clear and out into the main shipping channel. He said he would come back and show them where they could and couldn't go on the ship whilst aboard. Both of them decided to get some sleep as there was nothing else to do for the next six hours, nor indeed the next two weeks.

36

All smiles and feeling energised for the day ahead, Donald Lewis MP drove out of his London flat's secure car park ready for another day in Parliament and ran straight into a storm of flashing cameras and what seemed like a hundred reporters, but was probably closer to ten or eleven, trying to crowd around his Bentley, shouting things like, "Is it true you have been taking money from China?" Or. "Are you passing financial information to Beijing?" He slowly managed to get his car away from the reporters without running anyone down and while some stood on the pavement talking into cameras, others packed up furiously to chase after him like a cat chasing a mouse.

He placed a call to Kyle Greenwood's mobile and was met with a 'this number is not recognised' message. His mind was racing as he drove down Cromwell Road passing the Natural History Museum. He tried Kyle's number again just in case he had made an error, but the result was the same. After turning off St Margaret Street and clearing the security check, he noticed both the Home Secretary and the Foreign Secretary walking towards his car as he parked. He scrambled out as if he was going to do a runner but was as keen to speak to them as they were to him.

"Bloody press has made some garbage up from somewhere, I'm assuming by the bloody riot outside my flat this morning."

Kathleen Kingsley the Home Secretary passed him a copy of The Daily Telegraph as Sir Jacob Underhill, the Foreign Secretary, said,

"Don, you are so up to your neck if this shit proves correct."

Lewis took the paper with the front-page headline, 'Tory MP sells out to China.' There was also a picture of him shaking hands with Li Feng, a member of the Chinese Full Politburo and currently Director of the General Office.

"That was at a state reception! Jacob, you were there as well," Lewis emphasised as if trying to pass the buck.

"It's not just the picture, Donald."

Kathleen held up another newspaper, this time it was The Daily Mirror, showing a cartoon caricature of Donald Lewis sitting on a pile of cash and waving the 'Five Star Red Flag' of China.

"But this is all a made-up pile of rubbish! You need to ask my assistant, Greenwood, he will confirm this is all twaddle."

His voice was beginning to sound a little more pleading.

"Mr Greenwood, we haven't been able to locate yet; it seems he has gone underground. You see, this isn't just what the newspaper claims, a full investigation was initiated as soon as the information was leaked late last night, and the Parliamentary Commissioner has also received evidence of financial irregularities linked to you."

Donald Lewis bumbled and waffled his innocence as he was led into the building. In a small boardroom away from the normal parliamentary activities he was shown to a seat in front of a panel of five other MPs already seated, three from his party, one from the Lib Dems and a Labour MP who, as soon as Donald saw him, felt like he had just been kicked in the balls. Nick Clement never made eye contact at that point as he was reading through the six or seven A4 pages of information that had been passed to the newspapers, detailing what Donald Lewis had supposedly been up to.

There was one chair in the middle of the panel which was unoccupied, ready for the Parliamentary Commissioner who entered the room about five minutes after Lewis had sat down. Frances Santinelli was as English as a red rose; her name was the result of marrying an Italian Vineyard owner, following a quick romance after meeting at a charity event. She had studied law and sociology in her early years, making her way up through various organisations, both in England and other Commonwealth countries. Her husband had moved to London when they had married and now managed his vineyard in Tuscany from their large, eight-bedroomed house by the River Thames in Buckinghamshire, using his family villa as their retreat when needed for holidays or breaks.

"Donald Lewis, I am sure you now understand why you are here and that the basics, shall we say, have been highlighted to you by both the Home and Foreign Secretaries?"

"Yes, I am, but…"

Before he could continue, Frances raised her hand, cutting him off at once. "I will get straight to the point to make things clearer for you." She paused and poured a glass of water from the jug positioned in front of her. "Because of the nature of these allegations and after speaking to both the Prime Minister and the Attorney General, it has been decided to hand all the allegations, information and evidence we have received to the Metropolitan Police to investigate and decide if a criminal case should be raised."

Again, Donald Lewis went to say "but" and was in the process of standing, when the Commissioner again raised her hand and as he sat back down, she added,

"At this time, I reinforce that these are only investigations and I have been assured you are not under arrest. You are, however, suspended from the House pending investigations but are free from your home to continue constituency work and you will be expected to cooperate fully."

A member of the internal security staff led Donald Lewis out and back to his car. He didn't drive back to his Kensington flat, even to pick up any personal items or clothing, but headed out of London towards his reclusive farmhouse in Cambridgeshire, still reeling from what had just happened in the last few hours.

37

Apart from the single security guard at the main reception, monitoring all the CCTV cameras, the only two people in the building that Tuesday night were Emerson and Danny.

"Any news from Danielle on how things are going?"

Emerson had a glass of 'Emerald Isle' Irish whiskey between his hands which he was rolling from side to side, and he didn't look up as he spoke as if transfixed by the glow of the liquid which at over the two million he had paid for at auction was worth looking at a bit longer.

"Only a short report that she is bored as hell. Williams is a pain in the ass, and this is the worst cruise she's been on."

Danny wasn't drinking alcohol but did have a glass cup of iced tea which was going down a lot faster than Emerson's.

"She did say that the food was ok, but the captain doesn't want to have anything to do with them," Danny added.

"The captain may not like it, but the shipping company's owners have been rewarded sufficiently to carry out this request."

Emerson took another small sip then put the glass down and suddenly focused on Van Bloche.

"Right, Danny, I want you to go over again the plan for this weekend."

Danny put his cup down and began detailing a list of tasks and times, beginning from early Saturday morning with a private jet being prepared, fuelled and ready to leave from Farnborough Airport for Sunday morning. He explained that from 20:00 on Saturday, he would release all the security staff and take over until he got the order that the operation was complete.

Emerson interjected, "The clean-out phase."

Danny picked up his cup and finished his iced tea.

"The combustible solutions are in place in the basement, and I will need about an hour or two at most after all the security has left to set up ignition and fire spread equipment, place the extra flame boosts and links to the upper floors."

"What chemicals will you use to make it look like an accident?"

"The initial accelerant will be Glyphosate in liquid form."

"What is it?"

"We have it flagged as a weed killer stored on site, and I am going to have it rigged to be finely dispersed using a couple of small paint spray machines positioned between the basement and ground floor and a few well-placed fans which with the air movement produced, should create an explosive mixture right through the building."

"How will you start the fire?"

"It will be done on a countdown as we leave the building, but it is critical we get away before it takes hold because this stuff gives off poisonous gases in fires."

Danny continued to explain how he would wedge a system of fire doors open, using thin but strong cardboard props that as the fire flowed should last long enough to ensure the fire spread throughout quickly. He also explained that with the intensity in the basement, he was expecting the main structural parts of the building to fail which would add weeks, if not months, to any investigation.

"Sir, what of Kimmy when he has completed his role?"

"I think it's best if the fire is blamed on someone, don't you? But make sure he's alive when we leave, without any bullet holes or other injuries that make it suspicious."

Emerson stood, swallowed the last sip of whiskey and said, "I think we are just about ready to finish this thing off."

38

Traffic had been light for Chris Daniels who was driving a silver Mercedes Sprinter panel van, borrowed from a small lock-up garage near North Road in Islington. As they passed Ashford Hospital, he was feeling pleased with this latest bonus job that was going to be most profitable.

"Lenny, this could be the best one yet."

"What was the low-down with the Intel on it?"

Andrews replied, sitting with his arms folded, eyes closed but listening to every word.

"Hamin had been given word from his Turkish contact that he was shifting a double load out in a large order of car parts that have passed through Istanbul Airport from Japan."

"Where are we going to store it all between getting it shifted? That last lot wasn't appreciated by my old lady, filling up the hallway and front room for nearly two weeks."

Chris Daniels let out a little chuckle to himself, remembering the story Lenny had told him of how his wife had gone mad at the sight of box after box of dodgy Benson and Hedges and Dunhill cigarettes cluttered all around the house when she came in from working her night shift in a taxi firm's control room. It wasn't the fact that all the stuff was knocked off, it was the fact that Lenny had said she couldn't have even a single packet for herself.

"Don't worry, fella, the gear will stay in the lock-up van until we get it moved along the chain. You see, I made a deal with Benny Evans that all the while I keep the van he can do as many crooked MOTs as he likes."

"I bet Taff was happy with that arrangement."

Lenny had opened his eyes and looked at Daniels with a wide grin on his face.

"He couldn't give me the keys quick enough."

Daniels drove on down the Southern Perimeter Road, did a loop around, came back up then turned into Sealand Road before turning left into Southampton Road East. A hundred yards or so down the road he slowed and waited for a torch to flash from a window of one of the many cargo units based around the airport.

"There's Yuseff."

As the van got closer, an electric loading door began to rise. Daniels swung the van around and reversed into the unit and as soon as the front was clear, the loading door started to lower again. Both men got out and shook hands with Yuseff who had already moved the shipment into place using some pallet trucks.

"How many total Yuseff?"

"240 total boxes, 120 of Lambert and Butlers and 120 of Marlboroughs; each box has 100 cartons."

"Blimey, that's over a quarter of a mil!" Andrews sounded like an excited kid in a free sweet shop, and as he looked at Daniels, was rewarded with an 'I told you so' wink.

"The same method, Yuseff, we will shift them then split it three ways."

Yuseff nodded and in the back of his mind, he had already decided that after he got his share for this job, he would be getting out of England as quickly and as quietly as possible, then go and find another place somewhere in Europe to invest in another shady business on his way to a fruitful and enriched lifestyle.

They began to load the boxes from the pallets into the van, completely oblivious of the group of armed officers monitoring their actions from a Swissport Cargo Unit office just around the corner, from hidden cameras in the unit that had been secretly placed a few days before.

The last box was put in the van and the back doors closed as Lenny Andrews said he needed to take a leak and he headed to the toilet at the back of the unit. Daniels started the van as Yuseff operated the loading door, just as Lenny reappeared. It was Yuseff who noticed the large freight truck first, pulling onto the front apron of the unit and his animal instincts suddenly took hold as he noticed two more vans following behind it. He ducked under the door as it was still going up and ran.

"What the fuck is he up to?" Daniels said as Andrews got in the van and closed the door.

"I don't know but this doesn't look good."

Lenny grabbed the door handle to open just as the truck came to a stop right across the loading door about a metre away and the two vans went to either end. Doors flew open and black-clad, face-covered armed response officers ran in, pointing Heckler and Koch machine pistols at the two men in the van. There were no sudden movements from Daniels and Andrews; for all their acts of ill gain, they knew any false move would end badly for both of them.

"Williams will get us out of it if we say we are working undercover." Those were the last words from Andrews before the doors were opened and they were dragged out, bundled to the ground and plastic ties bound their hands behind their backs.

Yuseff had managed to get across Southern Perimeter Road in one go; by some miracle, the timing was perfect to avoid getting hit by traffic. He crossed the footbridge into Bedfont Road just as another van appeared out of Clare Road and a dog handler quickly got out and opened the back to retrieve an Alsatian dog.

Yuseff heard some shouts to stop and was just yards from entering some thick undergrowth by Clevland Park when he heard the barking. He found a gap by some small trees and bushes and a fence and began working away to squeeze through. The dog handler, realising Yuseff's struggle, decided not to release the dog but began a quick walk with it on a lead to the point where he had seen him go in and radioed up for the other dog van being used in support to head into Northumberland Close. The second dog handler was joined by one of the vans from the unit with some of the armed response team. The first dog handler had followed the route taken by Yuseff and the dog had easily picked up the scent, so, Sgt Sally 'Bolt' Holt was confident it was only a matter of time.

Yuseff had got to the back of some properties looking out onto Clare Road when the number of trees and bushes had become like a wall of thorns.

He knew he couldn't go any further, he knew it would be pointless to try and fight and turned around with a look of defeat and trudged towards the sounds of the dogs.

39

Unusually, it was Bob who had been first to take a seat out in the garden of the Lord Nelson and was halfway through his Guinness when George showed up with two more pints. This time there were no backpacks or rucksacks, and Bob had a small pad and pen only. George put both pints on the table and as he sat down, said,

"You aren't going to believe what I found out today."

Bob was raising his glass and stopped to look at George and put his glass back down.

"Am I going to like it?"

"Witch Williams bullyboys have been arrested."

"To do with the fires?"

"No, that's where it gets interesting."

George told Bob how he had bumped into an old mate from SO15, and as good mates did, told him that he had been on a special op to bring in a couple of bent coppers, linked to a big smuggling ring through Heathrow from Turkey. He hadn't been given any names or specifics about the job but from the details given on the two coppers, a quick check on station rosters and an IOPC team that, as he put it had been tearing down the big house and some of the outer Met stations, it had become fairly obvious.

"I assume from the big house you mean the Yard?"

"Yep."

"And has Williams been linked?"

"Not as far as I know so far, but I'm pretty sure they will."

"If they dig deep enough, they'll also rake up Sykes in this barrel of turds."

Bob picked up his second pint and said, "Cheers," to George before taking another sip to which George raised his glass and nodded a return 'cheers,' taking a big gulp.

"Do we hold off for this Sunday morning?" Bob asked only to gauge George's view.

"I still think we go, Bob, it may be that we uncover some more stuff that can add flames to the fire if you pardon the pun."

"In that case, I had better explain what I've found out so far for our entrance plan."

"Don't worry about the CCTV, I'll have my box of tricks again to make it play up at the right moments."

"The first point of access by the perimeter fence will be the toughest but I am hoping that the car fire stunt you pulled off has weakened the fencing because I took a drive past earlier and it hasn't been repaired or replaced yet."

"Cutting tools needed?" George asked more to see if they required anything special.

"I don't think so, the heat of that fire was substantial and hopefully long enough to have made it brittle enough for us to bend with some technical adjustment or brute force to give us access but I will have a backup plan."

"What's the backup if brute force isn't enough?"

"I've acquired a hydraulic hand pump set of cutting jaws from a station for a few hours, thanks to a good friend."

"Not off a front-line truck I hope?"

"No, it's from their old store of equipment used for training and backup."

"Right, Bob, before you continue, get a couple more beers, I'm a tad parched."

With their glasses replenished, Bob took out his notepad and explained that from the plans and information he had seen, at the back of the unit was a diesel tank that fed two large generators. The room had external access padlocked which he knew George could handle but Bob had picked up on the fact there was an access point that fed cabling down to the basement.

"Is it big enough?" George asked.

"I'm banking on the original gap being large enough and the fire stopping, which should have been put in place has probably been done badly with cheap materials and hopefully substandard or basic foam compounds which we can dissolve, using some industrial lacquer thinner."

"And if not?"

"If not, we may have to do a bit of digging or knock on the front door."

George spluttered as he sipped his Guinness looking at Bob with a worried look as if to say are you for real? Picking up on his reaction, Bob smiled a childish grin and explained it to him.

"A few years back, I carried out some inspections on some of the original units on the estate and the fire stopping was so shoddy, in some cases non-existent, and this unit was originally built by the same firm."

"No inspection completed," George said to himself more than to Bob.

"No inspection completed," Bob reaffirmed.

They chatted about a timeline once in the building, what they would be looking for and their exit plan if detected by the security guard. At this point, they decided that whatever they found they would need to pass all their information to the right agency to act on and deal with. George thought about it briefly and explained that outside of the Met, their only option probably was MI5 and that he had a contact who might be able to help, and also could go direct to the Director General if the information was substantial and proven. At least that way the ball could start rolling under someone else's responsibility and not with their heads in the firing line.

40

Heather Smallwood sat in one of the conference rooms at New Scotland Yard with four members of her team, who were taking turns to give updates on the information and details uncovered about the serving police officers and a large Turkish tobacco smuggling ring. She was making notes of the next tasks she would be handing out and to whom. She paused as the last remark filtered through her head and looking up, she spoke directly across the large oakwood table to Samir Daksh.

"Are you sure, Samir, they are the only two?"

"Yes, Ma-am. Instead of trying to find the links here, I spoke to a friend of mine in Ankara in their National Intelligence Organisation."

"And is the information credible?"

"Hakan couldn't give me the complete story, but he told me that they have an undercover operative in the ring who has been feeding back the main players for months now, prior to a large, planned response when as he put it, all the tentacles have been identified across a number of European countries."

"And how can we be sure Andrews and Daniels are the only ones, from this information received?"

"The sum of our conversation was that the London contacts from the airport handover man were a pair of rogue coppers freelancing."

"Can we substantiate this through any financial transactions, Jamie?" She looked to Samir's left where a mid-thirties man in a suit and with his hair in a ponytail, had a laptop in front of him. He looked up.

"Boss, I've found nothing in any banking details to tie anyone else in which means that it's all cash movements."

"So, we can't be a hundred per cent, but the sources are supporting it." Heather's response was said as a statement and not directed at anyone specific.

"One thing though, boss, if they have been raking it in, there have to be some large amounts of cash stored somewhere."

Jamie's remark was as obvious to all the team sitting around the table, but it was also raised as a possible request to carry out a search of the suspects' addresses and any other places of interest.

"I think I'll have to have a conversation with the commissioner and see how we play that line of inquiry at this time."

There was a knock at the door and Thomas Fawling entered the room. He decided to stand at the head of the table before addressing the group seated.

"Preliminary interviews have been conducted with Andrews and Daniels and they have both stated that they have been working an undercover operation for Georgina Williams in busting open a smuggling operation."

Fawling looked directly at Heather Smallwood and answered the next question before it even came out of her mouth.

"We haven't been able to verify this, as Williams appears to have vanished."

The silence didn't last long, and, in these situations, Thomas Fawling was used to shouting and swearing and often it was him who flew into a rage but Heather Smallwood, as her team had come to realise, was more the quiet assassin who always used knowledge, experience, and a calm way to get results or chastise underlings or equals.

"Firstly, Tom, how long before she was discovered absent or are we saying missing?"

"The best case is the last twenty-four hours, worst case three days."

"And do we know if there is anything suspicious about her disappearance, forcibly removed or worse, or has she done a runner?"

"I have sent some officers over to check her apartment but at this point, there are no clear ideas as to where she has gone."

As soon as Fawling had dropped the bombshell, Jamie had begun tapping keys quietly on his laptop and within a few minutes, looked up at Heather Smallwood.

"There has been no Georgina Williams out of the airports of London in the last three days, Boss."

Fawling looked at Jamie with a 'how did you do that so quickly?' look. Jamie smiled back and explained,

"In this job, there is often a need to find people moving in and out of airports, so I had a friend build a program for me sanctioned by MI5 and MI6 which allows me to specifically search passengers in and out."

"And they are ok with that?"

"They have access to see who we are looking at and if it is a person of interest to them or one of their own, they call the boss who advises me to proceed or delete," he was looking at Heather as he spoke.

"Tom, what is your gut feeling on the undercover operation story?"

"It's possible, but until we find Williams or establish her whereabouts, I honestly don't know."

"If this whole thing is a genuine police operation that changes our involvement, we will still investigate because something has gone wrong with proper police protocols."

"I agree, Heather, if this was a genuine op, I or the commissioner should have been informed at the outset to sanction or deny it."

There was another knock at the door. Fawling walked over

and opened it to a plainclothes detective sergeant. Heather couldn't hear the mutterings between them but did pick up Fawling saying "shit". He closed the door and returned to stand at the head of the table.

"Williams' apartment is tidy with no sign that anything bad has happened. However, some of the wardrobes and drawers show signs of clothes being taken with no suitcases found in the place."

"She's done a runner but where to and is she alone in this?" said Jamie.

Heather made a couple of notes on the pad in front of her, tore out the pages and handed one to Jamie. He read it and immediately closed his laptop, picked up all his stuff and left without saying anything. The other she gave to Samir simply read *'check back through your Turkish connection and see if Williams surfaces there'* Samir also nodded and as he stood said,

"I'll get onto it now boss; we should get a reply back fairly quickly."

The other two members of her team in the room were asked politely to leave. Jenna Dulley who had been making a transcript of the meeting and Lawrence Booker fondly known as the 'arranger' because to complete some tasks he would sort out transport, meetings and ensure people were where they had to be and when; both stood and left.

"Take a seat, Tom, I need to ask you another favour."

As the door was closed leaving the two alone, Smallwood sat back a little in her chair.

"Tom, can you as part of your investigation of Daniels and Andrews order a search of their homes and any other places like a garage, allotment shed or any place they could stash money?"

"Of course, but it will need to be done right because if this were a genuine op, we would look bloody stupid."

"Agreed but also if it was genuine any cash would have been

declared and I assume held securely?"

"Under normal circumstances, yes."

"I'll leave it to you but let me know if you find anything of value as to what we do next."

As Thomas Fawling stood, he asked if she would meet him for lunch tomorrow where he could update her with things but in a more relaxed manner, which meant he was also apologising for what was feeling like a massive Met cock-up.

41

Back in his office, Bob was working through some crewing levels for the fire investigation teams. It was normal that through the summer months officers and crews would be using up their summer leave and Bob was always given the projected deficiencies or low numbers to look over, not because he wanted to micro-manage the team managers, but in some cases where other personnel had requested transfers or secondments into the FIT teams, he could give them a little taster knowing that some would thrive and some would decide it's not for them and at least this way the service could find the right people before investing large amounts of money in their training.

Jane knocked on the door and entered with a fresh cup of tea and as she put it down, she said,

"I've just been up to the big offices to pass some internal post and reports and while talking to the Dep's PA, I saw Sykes in the corridor."

"I'm fairly sure there's something else coming, Janey."

"He looked awful, Bob, like he hadn't slept in days."

Jane had Bob's attention and he put his paperwork down and picked up the fresh cup of tea.

"It wasn't just his look, he also seemed twitchy like a rabbit caught in the headlights."

"Maybe he's had a roasting from the old man."

"Just saying he looked like a bag of crap and a nervous wreck."

"Do me a favour, Janey, see if you can access the resources attendance record and check on Drayton would you?"

Jane left, closing the door behind her, and Bob sat back, put his tea down, stretched his hands behind his head and closed his eyes for a minute or two.

Jane came back in, snapping him out of his trance-like moment.

"He's not in the resources department attendance records."

"Where's he gone then?"

"Moved to Dagenham working the tech op support stuff."

"That sounds like a shafting from what he was doing?"

"More than that, I took a peek at the transfer requests and he's looking to move out."

"How did you find that little bombshell?"

"Only for you to know but obviously I have worked in other roles before I moved in here with you lot, and some of the access granted to me has stayed, or should I say I forgot to relinquish some of my perks."

"Good stuff, thanks, Janey."

Jane left and Bob's mind started working overtime trying to make sense of Sykes' current state and his obvious ex-sidekick's sudden fall from grace.

He knew that both were involved in the cover-ups of at least two fatal fires and also Sykes' pressure exerted on an Incident Commander not to carry out his duties on the fireground. What he lacked was solid evidence and a way of linking it all together. He finished his tea and headed out onto Albert Embankment, crossed Lambeth Bridge, walked into Victoria Tower Gardens and called his wife for a daily catch-up of what she'd been up to with the grandchildren, where they'd been and how much he was missing her. The last thing he said before saying goodbye was that hopefully everything would be sorted after the weekend, and he would be back to normal duties.

Bob did not want to concern his wife and had made a story up of some late working from the office and possibly a few all-night shifts to fine-tune working practices. Sally knew his work sometimes disrupted life, usually only in short stints so any excuse to visit their daughter and grandchildren in Devon was always welcomed. Bob said goodbye and as he put his phone in his pocket, he found himself looking up at the Burghers of Calais statue. Ironic, he thought as it represented the idea of freedom from oppression which seemed appropriate at that moment. Bob smiled, relaxed a little and began walking back to his office thinking that the statue and the story of the siege of Calais in 1347, during the Hundred Years War may be getting re-enacted very soon.

42

The day was warm and clear and the riverboat moved calmly down the Thames as Thomas Fawling began updating Heather over the last twenty-four hours. He had chosen to treat her to lunch from the Bateaux London, a superb restaurant that offered various dining experiences based on the Victoria Embankment. This was not only as a way of apologising but also on the river they wouldn't be disturbed, and even though the subject matter would be sour the lunch would be pleasant.

Heather knew that with such a splendid offer of lunch, the news she would hear wasn't going to be great, but she would get the job done one way or another.

"Both Daniels and Andrews were interviewed again after our meeting yesterday and stuck to their story of an undercover operation, sanctioned by Williams."

"And still no idea of her whereabouts?"

"Nothing, almost like she just disappeared."

"Because we were running out of time on holding them without charging them, I spoke to the Commissioner about your suggested search."

Heather nodded as she took a sip of iced water with lemon.

"And this morning, we searched their home addresses, one old garage lock-up and a storage unit that Andrews rents."

"I've a feeling the searches didn't produce anything."

"Not a thing, apart from in Andrews' unit we found a couple of boxes of fake Rolex watches, the sort you buy in Thailand for twenty dollars and shift to gullible punters in pubs and clubs for anything from fifty to a hundred pounds."

"Not a great result then."

Fawling picked up his own glass, took a gulp of refreshing lemon iced water and as he put his glass down, smiled and cleared his throat like a judge about to pass sentence.

"Not entirely, one of the team at the lock-up raid found a written receipt for an old transit Luton van which we managed to trace to a scrap yard just up north of Burnt Oak."

"And going by the grin on your face, you found something?"

"The van was tucked away in the corner of the yard and the owner was being paid a small fee to make sure it was left alone. He also said that the two guys occasionally came in the evening to drop off, or pick up stuff from it."

There was a pause in the conversation as a waiter topped up their glasses and served the appetizers. Both had chosen a pasta salad bowl with a sprinkling of mussels.

"We called a forensic team in before we moved on the van and just as a precaution, the inspector heading up the team had a firearms and bomb expert do a quick check to make sure there were no surprises waiting."

They both took a couple of small bites from their lunch before Thomas continued,

"The van was like an Aladdin's cave, boxes stuffed with cash, boxes of smuggled tobacco and gold jewellery that's probably been stolen."

Heather had a look of triumph but also knew the crap that was about to hit Thomas and the Met.

"The forensic team pulled plenty of prints and along with all the stuff we wanted to find, there were other things that are a bit odd."

"Such as?"

"Keys from some stolen cars that have been found burnt out recently, and we found a couple of fire reports that must have been taken from the LFB, but I don't know how or why."

"Have you contacted fire about it?"

"Not yet, we are still going through things at our end, but I will talk to them early next week after we squeeze those two, now that we have some leverage."

They took another couple of minutes eating their lunch and as was fashionable, Heather left a small amount on the side of her plate. She took another sip of water, pushed her chair back a little and picked her bag up from under the table by her feet. Opening it, she took out a couple of folded A4 sheets of paper and passed them to Thomas.

"Jamie has good contacts in various agencies and managed to get some access to the capital's camera network. The images are not great but he's pretty sure that's Williams leaving her apartment dressed to go jogging at 05:03."

"I would say so," Fawling agreed.

"The others show her trail until we lose her under a rail bridge."

"And these images?" Thomas held up the second page.

"Jamie picked up on something odd in a couple of the shots, so went back through the route from additional cameras from adjoining roads on her route. He found that one particular car was seen making loops around her as she walked."

"We can't rule out foul play then?"

Heather took another folded page out of her bag and passed it over.

"Jamie decided to keep going back in time on a couple of cameras directed towards her apartment."

"Well, that seems to settle that argument then."

The image showed the same car outside Williams' apartment picking up a couple of suitcases.

43

George picked Bob up around the corner from his house just after 10:30, as the evening light began to fade, and they headed for their first holding point at the Hounslow train station car park. George parked in a corner under some trees, took an iPad from his backpack and opened up a program which showed the unit from the camera he had installed days before. They sat there for thirty minutes and watched, with the most interesting thing being seagulls landing on the roof.

George placed the pad on the back seat, started the car and headed for the next holding point which was on the industrial estate where the unit was, but well-hidden at the opposite end. Again, he took up his iPad and began watching. There were still a couple of cars parked, one George recognised as the black Mercedes from the previous stakeout and another, a Jaguar F-Type in British Racing Green.

"Looks like the boss is working late," Bob said.

"The boss isn't the problem, that other car belongs to the hired muscle."

They sat watching for twenty minutes then noticed someone get in the black Mercedes and exit through the main gate. George closed the iPad down and started the car.

"Looks like the biggest problem has gone," he said. "It's now or never Bob, you good to go?"

"As ready as I'm going to be but what about the head honcho?"

"I reckon he'll be in his office on the top floor, so hopefully we can clear most of the building without being noticed and if we are, we run."

He parked the car between a couple of empty trailers outside a unit about a hundred yards west of Scientia Global. They were both dressed in dark clothing and as George opened the boot of another borrowed vehicle, this time a classic Volvo S40 which had more dents than a golf ball and likely had replaced its plates more times than a Greek restaurant, they removed their backpacks and closed the boot.

They moved north towards the edge of the industrial estate and used some scrubland to move within about thirty yards of the unit. George stopped, knelt down and took out an electronic box that was shaped a bit like a small alarm clock radio. He switched it on and watched as a sequence of numbers began a random dance across the screen, occasionally pausing before starting again.

"What does that thing do, George and how do you know it's working?"

"I have a good friend in the FBI who owed me a favour or two from my early days in SO15 and some joint work we did, so one day I asked him about getting past CCTV and security cameras and he sent me this in a diplomatic pouch."

George picked up the box and showed Bob the screen.

"All these numbers are frequencies which are being located within only a short distance, up to about two hundred yards max, and as it finds them, it interrupts them and sends back a pulse on the same frequency which freezes the camera or scrambles it."

"How does it cover us?"

"The principle is that it picks the strongest signals to the box, such as the nearest cameras to us and it will freeze the pictures. Then as we move out of range, it disrupts it a bit like when lightning makes your TV go off briefly."

"What about other cameras?"

"It will go through a sequence of counting out with other signals, so in turn, other cameras in our arc will react the same."

"How long will it work for?"

"What I will say is that we still need to move quicker than a hedgehog and hope that point at the fence you said will work for us."

George had a wide grin as he put the box in his backpack, and they began the move to the perimeter fence.

The spot was easy to locate from the scorched grass and blistered paint on the metal fence. Bob knelt down and with gloves on, moved his hand up from the bottom thin metal slat and found what he was looking for. The car fire had twisted some of the fence slats and at the hottest point of the fire, about three feet up, some had twisted and buckled a little in the heat. He took a small jemmy bar out of his bag and levered one to the left a bit; as it moved, the buckled point crumpled easily, allowing him to pull it up. He did this with three more slats quickly and both of them stepped through the gap. Before moving off, Bob took out what looked like four strips of cloth painted the same colour as the fence, each had a small fishing weight at the bottom, and he taped them to the fence to cover the gap.

"The camera should see a complete fence, but I am banking that nobody walks the external perimeter at night."

They moved up to the wall at the rear of the unit and the door to the diesel tank room which was secured by a container padlock, not the normal cheap ones you get from a hardware store. Not that it mattered to George who after a quick look, took some picking tools out from the side pocket of his black cargo trousers and picked the lock almost instantly and turned to Bob.

"I do like it when these things are nice and new, so much easier than an old rusty thing."

They took the padlock with them and moved into the store, closing the door behind them. The diesel store had been constructed as part of the main unit but was in effect a separate room attached. It was immediately evident to Bob that they had constructed the main walls with a high fire-resisting material, both inside and out and established probably as much as two-hour protection. This worried him a little if the additional work inside had included any decent fire stopping. There were two 10,000-litre diesel tanks, bunded with an electric pump in between that was fed by two pipes, one from each tank, which was then pumped towards the back of the compartment.

"That's a lot of fuel being stored," said George.

"There must be some pretty mean generators around here somewhere," Bob replied.

George looked at his watch.

"Took us less than seven minutes to here."

"Now let's have a look to see if they have done a shoddy job on that other stuff you said about."

44

Kimmy had been watching the screen for just over two hours when Emerson came out and sat next to him to check the progress.

"Any concerns so far, Kimmy?"

"No, Sir, the run time is slower, but I have fed extra links through quite a few extra countries, schools, businesses and transport hubs to give added protection."

"Let me know when you reach the main file, so I can tell you what to download."

"Yes, Sir."

Emerson walked back into his office, closed the door and sat down, taking a mobile out of his desk.

"Is everything set, Danny?"

"Yes, Sir, the plane is all set, and I am just going to pick up a couple of things from the safe house, check it's clean then return."

"Good. When you get back, if Kimmy has been successful and the download is near completion, I have decided to leave while you tidy everything up here."

"Yes, Sir, I should be back within the next hour or so."

Emerson cut the call off and began taking specific items and paperwork out of his desk, putting them into a briefcase. He walked over to the walnut unit that had the imported Italian coffee machine on and opened the door, revealing a safe below. He opened it with a thumb scanner and taking a medium-sized duffel bag began emptying the contents into it, including various currencies of money in note form; there were pounds, dollars some euros and four million of Neuvo Sol in 100s and 200s soles. He took two small pouches of cut diamonds and put them in his briefcase. The last thing from the safe were two passports, one for the Kingdom of the Netherlands and the other a diplomatic Bahrain passport, secured for some jobs well done in his earlier days. His South African passport was in his briefcase, which he hoped would be the only one needed for his initial travel requirements. When the safe was empty, he took some logbooks from his desk, placed them on the shelves and left the door open; this would remove some more details of the operation when the fire took hold and he thought would also point to a robbery.

He looked at his watch, it was twenty-past two in the morning. He got another coffee and sat back down, mentally going through things again, crossing off tasks in his head and checking what else needed to be done. He glanced through the glass at Kimmy who was still fixed on the screen. It was a shame to waste such a talent he thought, but he wanted a fall guy left behind and there was always the chance if the blame went well, he could return one day, should an opportunity arise for the right reason.

45

Bob couldn't believe their luck when he saw where the fuel lines ran down into the basement. Because they'd installed a series of cut-off and safety valves to the fuel lines, they had made a gap of about a square metre which had been filled up with some cheap expansion foam. Bob took a small metallic flask out of his bag and poured it in spots around where the foam met the concrete. The fluid slowly began eating through the foam and after about ten minutes, Bob placed his boot on the centre mass of the foam and applied some pressure. Soon the foam made a low crunching noise and began to give way and surprised him even more when suddenly it fell to the basement floor below, leaving the remains of what was a mere two inches of foam used to create the impression of a sixty-minute fire barrier.

"I thought it would be shoddy but not that bad."

George started to remove a rope from his bag and replied,

"Shoddy to you, great news to me."

He moved back into the compartment to tie the rope to a large steel bracket on one of the fuel tanks. Bob looked at the rope as George fed it down into the hole, to the bottom of the basement. George had seen the look and had picked up that Bob was looking at a fire service general purpose line.

"I have some contacts as well in the brigade."

"Glad it was the long line," Bob said.

George went first and after a short look around, he came back to the bottom of the line and signalled for Bob to join him. After Bob had reached the basement, George cleared the foam from the floor and moved the line that was hanging down to the back wall and snagged it in some cables, so it wasn't blatantly obvious in any camera's view, which seemed non-existent inside the building anyway, or just in case a security guard glancing in on a walk around, noticed it. This again would be slim, based on the rear of the basement having a large concrete pillar right in the way, which had obscured their route in. As he made his way back into the room, he picked up on the concern on Bob's face.

"Problem?" George asked.

"I'd say so, take a look at those barrels and where they're located." Bob pointed to the barrels in the basement.

"Glyphosate, that's weed killer right?"

"Yep, a shit-load of it which firstly isn't right, and each of these barrels have been put right by the generators and their fuel lines, which can only mean that someone is making a firebomb."

George went and took a closer look at a couple of the barrels and after a quick check over and all around them, returned to where Bob was standing so as not to talk too loudly.

"There are no detonators of any sort on them."

"Not yet, or they're hoping for something else to get started first before these bad boys become involved."

"Best we get a chivvy on then Bob, so we can wrap this up and dump it into someone else's lap."

George went first and headed towards the stairs leading up from the basement. As he got to the bottom step, he noticed another barrel tucked to the side but this one had a small box on top with a power cable running to a socket. George carefully lifted the box off revealing a medium-sized spray gun with its paint supply tube running down into the barrel. George put the cover back on and moved up the stairs, finding another barrel and spray gun on the landing between the two doors that opened onto the ground floor. George cracked it open a little and listened for a minute, before slowly opening it allowing them to move into a corridor which appeared to have a couple of storerooms off it. There was a door at each end of the short corridor, and they moved towards the one that would be at the back of the unit. Here they found a stairwell going up.

"I reckon we start on the first floor and work our way up," said Bob. "The ground is only going to be the reception and general stuff and if we don't find anything, check it then."

"Good to me," replied George.

The stairwell went up a little and half-turned before arriving at the first floor where they found a set of double doors. They slowly moved through one of the doors where they could see an open office area, which then fed into a small corridor with meeting rooms off it.

"You go left, George. I'll take the right and meet you at the end."

George nodded, and they set off. They didn't need to use torches as it seemed that half of the lights were left on and it was easy to see everything lying around on the workstations and desks. As they moved almost like a mirror image of each other, they picked up bits of paper or reports, but it seemed nothing found was of any use to them and they soon arrived at the end of the corridor where another set of doors opened out onto the main front stairwell.

"Back to the rear stairs and up to the next level, Bob, that way we keep away from the front of the building."

Bob nodded and at the same slow, but methodical pace, they moved back to where they had entered the first floor.

46

Kimmy stood up and raised his arm, signalling to Emerson that he had found something. As Emerson stood, he saw Danny's SUV approaching the gate and he thought to himself that was perfect timing. He walked out of his office and sat down next to Kimmy, looking at the screen he noted the first page of files.

"Scroll through the pages please."

Kimmy tapped the keyboard and after each one paused until Emerson saw what he was looking for.

"There that one, the overseas security deposits."

Kimmy accessed the file and it opened onto more pages of files, but each file had a reference code and country abbreviation. Emerson handed over another plug-in drive.

"Take this hard drive, open the locust program and download all of these into it."

"Yes, Sir."

As Emerson returned to his office, Danny Van Bloche exited the lift and walked past Kimmy, closing the door as he entered the office.

"All good, Danny?"

"Yes, Sir. The safe house is clear, and I have the equipment to prime the barrels and begin the countdown."

"Good, as soon as Kimmy completes the download, I will take the hard drive and meet you at the plane."

"Sir, what of Greenwood? He seems to have gone underground and without Danielle to assist, I haven't had time to locate him."

"Once we are out of here, and even if he does resurface, with all the scandal on Donald Lewis and his links to him, I don't think we need to worry too much. But what I will do is get something together to give to the media anonymously, maybe about cocaine-fuelled sex parties with the MP which will make him crawl back under a rock."

Kimmy stood up again and signalled to Emerson.

"Well, Danny, it looks like we shall soon have filled our pockets to the brim, thanks to the inept systems of the British Government and the generosity of foreign countries."

Danny allowed a smile to briefly flash on his face. They stood in unison and Emerson took a bottle of Louis Roederer champagne from another cabinet in his office and with three glasses, they walked out of the office to join Kimmy. He opened the bottle and poured two glasses, passing one to Kimmy and taking the other. He raised his glass and congratulated Kimmy on an exceptional job and took a gulp. As Kimmy took a mouthful, he closed his eyes, savouring the refreshing but unusual taste, but as he relaxed, he was suddenly hit by a wave of horror as Van Bloche took a firm grip around him and placed a cloth over his nose and mouth. Within two seconds, Kimmy had gone limp and a further five had him unconscious.

"I'll have mine on the plane, Sir, when we take off," Danny smiled.

Emerson returned to the office, placed the hard drive in the duffel bag and with his briefcase left, telling Danny not to be late. Danny had laid the now comatose North Korean on the floor and put a couple of cable ties on his hands and feet, in case he managed to regain consciousness before the next lot of chloroform was needed, just prior to the fire countdown. Then he returned to call the lift back up so he could go down to the car to get his equipment and head to the basement to begin his final tasks.

47

Both men had found nothing but a mirrored floor layout for the first and second floors. It seemed that most of the work areas were not being used and the few that were had very little, apart from some daily work reports and nothing with any names of interest to them. They began their steps up the stairwell to the top floor; as they got to the door, they suddenly became aware of the lift moving downwards.

"Perhaps that was the last one out," Bob whispered.

They moved to the door to access the last floor but instead of opening like all the others, this one was locked. George took a minute or so to pick the lock and as the door opened, he whispered,

"Makes you think they don't want people up here."

The door opened out onto a small landing, leading to another door which fed out into an open area similar in shape to the other floors. However, this one had them both fixated on all the computers and monitors as they moved into it. Suddenly, George felt Bob tap his shoulder and then pointed to what appeared to be a man's legs and feet sticking out from under a worktop in the adjoining room. George went first and as they rolled him over, he thought he recognised him from the pictures he had taken days earlier. Seeing he was breathing and not dead, he told Bob to check him out and moved on into the office.

Meanwhile, below them, Van Bloche had entered the top of the basement and began by first wedging the doors open, then uncovering the spray guns as he went down the stairs. He moved just inside the basement at the bottom of the stairwell and put down a briefcase-sized hard case and opened it to reveal some small timing clocks, wrapped with a small lump of plastic explosive on one side and on the other, a phosphorous stick. He taped the devices on the fuel pipes to the generators right up against the barrels. Checking his watch, he worked out the time he needed to move throughout the building, wedging open the other doors and enough time to be away from the building when the timers went off.

George had seen that the office had been cleared but was delighted to pick up some papers in the open safe and stuff them in his backpack, but his expression suddenly changed, glancing out of the window he saw the black SUV parked outside the entrance to the unit. Moving swiftly back to Bob who had dragged the unconscious man out from under the desk, cut the cable ties and checked him over. He looked up at George.

"Looks like he's been drugged or something, no injuries I can see."

"Good, but we've got company and I think it's time to get out of here. I need you to take my pack, also can you carry him on your own? I need to be ready for the bad guys, just in case."

Bob looked sceptical but knew George had to be ready for anything.

"I reckon I can drag him."

"Great, we are going the same way down, but I'll try and find another quick way out at ground level."

Initially, it was hard going for Bob to move the unconscious guy along the floor but when they got to the stairwell, thanks to gravity, momentum and a clean concrete floor, it became a little easier. George went down a floor first then signalled with a low call of, "Now!" for Bob to move down before clearing the next steps. They got down to the first-floor landing and Bob signalled to George for a quick thirty seconds to get his breath back, then both men looked at each other as a waft of a chemical smell drifted up the stairs. He nodded to George that he was ready to go again, and they both continued downwards, leaving about eight steps between them. As George got to the bottom, he spotted a figure coming through the wedged-open doors at the top of the basement steps and ran forward shouting to his friend,

"GO NOW, BOB!"

48

Danny was only surprised for a split second, but he had no chance to react as a fast-moving shape in black slammed into him, knocking him down the basement steps. Luckily for him, he had gone sideways and managed to slide more than tumble over and over. What he didn't expect was the black shape followed him down and was suddenly upon him, not hitting but putting pressure across his throat. He managed to force the arm off a little and got a half-punch to the aggressor's stomach which was met with a rough grunt. They both rolled over into the basement and Danny was suddenly reminded of the smell of Glyphosate filling the basement and the sound of the fans and spray guns mixing the atmosphere. He was now regretting the decision to leave his gun in the car but still felt this situation was something he could turn around with his experience and guile.

He managed another small punch to the gut and it was enough to allow him to shuffle back a little, then he tried to roll over onto his knees but just as he thought he was going to be clear and get to his feet, the shape came again dropping an elbow into the lower spine area. As the pain shot through him, he swung a leg around, catching his assailant on the side of the knee and stopping him in his tracks. Now he thought it was his turn to become the hunter but as he stood up the atmosphere was becoming unbearable from the mixture of weed killer and air being circulated around the basement and his mind shot back briefly to the timers he had set. The delay gave the shadowy figure time to move again, but not towards him, towards the stairs. Danny grabbed a barrel-opening bar from the top of one of the barrels and threw it, hitting the fleeing figure on the shoulder just as he got close to the bottom stair, sending him flying to the floor. He followed him rapidly, pouncing on him from behind and wrapping an arm around his neck. Now, thought Danny, I have another body for them to find and a perfect suspect for the fire.

He began squeezing to render the mysterious person unconscious and felt a slight sagging in his prey which gave him a rush of power. Just as he thought victory was his, he caught sight of another shadow, but before he could react, he felt a sudden blow to the side of his head and blacked out.

Bob grabbed George and managed to help him up the stairs and out by the main entrance door, where the other guy was still out of it on the ground.

"Fuck me, that was a close call, Bob, I thought I had him."

"Maybe you're getting too old for this shit, George," chuckled Bob.

"What did you hit him with anyway?" George spluttered as the fresh air got back into his lungs.

"You know that box of tricks you had for the cameras? Well, that seemed like the best thing at the time."

"Better wait here a minute then, while I make sure the cameras haven't picked us up, now or until we get clear of here."

George disappeared and came back less than forty-five seconds later.

"Someone else had already switched all the security stuff off and I've switched the gate to open permanently so we're good to get out of here."

"And this one, whoever he is?"

Bob was looking at the prone figure at their feet.

"He must be in on some of this mess, so let's take him and find a place of safety for now."

They decided to use the black Mercedes that had been left, not just because it was unlocked with the keys in, but also because Bob had told George that as he had carried him down all those steps and saved his arse, it was his turn to drag the guy to their car which was when George suggested plan B.

It was Bob who heard the first small pop noise from inside the building, just as they closed the back door with their new guest, but it was George who picked up on the noises next, and rapidly got in and started the engine, driving off as Bob was closing his door.

Seen from their mirrors, the building didn't explode like in the films. There was a series of rumbles and a surge of thick smoke, followed by orange waves that initially reached outwards, shattering windows before slowly withdrawing back into the building to begin its fiery ingestion of the unit.

They picked up the other car and George told Bob to follow him. They drove east for a while and Bob followed George onto Smugglers Way, where just as they passed the Western Riverside Waste Authority site at Wandsworth, George slowed down and stopped near some trees. Suddenly a young lady dressed in a black hoodie, black cargo trousers and Nike trainers stepped out from the cover. George got out and gave her a hug, before telling Bob to leave the car and get in with him. She replaced Bob in the S40 and disappeared as he got into the Mercedes.

"Before you ask, that was Petra, daughter of Matej Horvat and I'm her godfather."

"You mean Matej the Motor? I've heard of him," said Bob.

"Only the good stuff, I expect. He is a genuine guy but you just don't get on his wrong side. Anyway, the short version is I saved his life a few years back and we are sort of blood brothers and look out for each other where we can."

"That would also explain the transport supply over the recent days, and Petra?" Bob asked.

"She is more like a daughter to me and there isn't a thing with a steering wheel she can't drive; also, she could drink me and you under the table."

George began chuckling and drove on, heading to Bermondsey just as their guest began to stir a little.

49

Emerson felt something was wrong only five minutes after the time Danny was supposed to have arrived and decided to take off immediately. In all his years, Danny was always either early or bang on time, never late. So, he didn't want to waste time that could be precious and once up in the air, he would endeavour to find out where he was.

As the Gulfstream G650 climbed up to its flight path, Emerson first tried Danny's phone which came back as unobtainable. So, he started up a laptop in front of him and began searching news sites for the London area. He found nothing on local news and London fire incidents were often a few hours behind, before being shared on their website.

Something must have gone wrong, maybe the detonation went off early he thought, but quickly removed that idea. Danny was a specialist in explosives, it couldn't have been that. Maybe Kimmy had regained consciousness and surprised Danny somewhere in the building. But again, it seemed unlikely that a computer nerd could take down a trained killer. What was puzzling him was why the phone was unobtainable; then he suddenly remembered some of the programs he had access to.

The first program he tried was what he referred to as a leech tagging app, which enabled him to track mobile phones by attaching to all the phone operators' masts and signals and searching for the last position of a mobile when the number was entered in. It soon found the last active position of Danny's phone and gave the nearest postcode, which was at the Hounslow unit which he was assuming or hoping had been completely destroyed in a mystery fire by now.

At this point, he was positive that something had gone wrong but maybe just maybe, Danny's phone had been damaged or fallen out of his pocket during the operation, so he would wait a few hours before trying to find out more information on news or local websites. He closed down the laptop, took out his mobile and sent a message to Danielle Keller; it simply read 'GO TO MEXICO CITY WILL PICK YOU UP IN 14 HOURS'. He switched the phone off and reclined a little in the chair and while he was trying to think things over, with different scenarios both bad and good, he slipped into a light sleep.

He was suddenly woken by a slight jolt as the Gulfstream encountered a little turbulence and looking at his watch, was shocked to see he had slept for just over five hours. He stood up and stretched his legs, fixed a cold drink and sat back down restarting the laptop. He began first to revisit agency websites and local online news channels. After a few minutes, he came across a story currently running of a fatal fire at an industrial unit in Hounslow but there was very little detail in the story. Then he found the Hounslow Herald which had gone as far as to say *'one person dies in industrial unit fire'* which briefly lifted Emerson's hopes; that had to be Kimmy in the fire he thought.

As he was beginning to think Danny would find a way to contact him, he found another news site 'My London News' with a headline that simply read *'suspicious fatal fire at industrial unit body found in basement'*. Again, it started Emerson's mind racing through the what-ifs and buts. He again closed down the laptop and made his mind up to carry on to his next destination and sort things out from there, if Danny was ok, he would get word to Emerson or turn up eventually.

50

Bob and Kimmy had been talking for about an hour, sharing their life experiences and stories like new best friends. Two days ago, when Kimmy had regained consciousness, George had explained the events from earlier and how Bob had carried the Korean whizz kid from what would almost certainly have been his last place of employment. Kimmy, on hearing the story, had briefly broken down and hugged Bob and then assured them both he wouldn't run and would help as much as he could. And now they both had taken a window table in The Angel pub in Bermondsey, not far from a flat George had managed to borrow for a few days as a safe house.

It was approaching 2 o'clock when George walked in with a couple of people in tow. He introduced them as Tim Collins and Jeff Killick. They all shook hands and as the two new people joined them at the table, Tim remarked on the fantastic view out onto the Thames as George went to the bar and ordered three more drinks.

It was Tim who started the conversation.

"Firstly, it's great to meet you, Bob; George has told me a lot about you and the last few weeks; and Kimmy, I want to put you at ease, from what we have been told and the fact you are willing to assist us, we will try to do what we can for you in all this mess."

Kimmy just nodded at this point as George returned with two orange juices and a Guinness for himself.

Jeff Killick took a sip of juice and put his glass down and faced Bob first.

"Because of both the sensitivity of what has happened and the major agencies that are going to get involved, probably right up to the Prime Minister, I have suggested to Tim that we take this whole mess off you and if we can keep both you and George out of this as much as we possibly can."

"Works for me but will it be possible, based on what has gone on?" Bob asked.

Tim explained that he was going to approach the Director General and give him all the information they had, then with all the details given over, the decision would be made at the very top, but he was fairly sure things would work out ok.

"The thing is, gents, what has happened will basically embarrass the country and some of our foreign partners will move quickly to drop us in the shit if we don't sort this mess out," said Jeff, then looked at Kimmy. "Which is where you come in, Kim Son, or can I call you Kimmy?"

Kimmy nodded again and took a gulp of the organic beer Bob had recommended when they first entered, put his glass down and looked at both the MI5 men with a grin like a Cheshire cat. It was Tim this time that nearly choked on his juice on hearing Kimmy's next words,

"He won't be able to use it."

"What do you mean? He has downloaded all the files from the exchange," said Tim, regaining his composure.

"I had to be sure I was going to be a part of things and after Misha disappeared, I began to think I was next."

"Why didn't you come to us?" Jeff asked.

"The South African and his lapdog are people I did not want to cross."

"So, why can't he use the download?"

"I installed a Dokkaebi."

Jeff and Tim looked at each other as Bob and George both shrugged their shoulders, not being computer boffs and only ever using them when they had to. Tim was up with a lot of computer hack stuff and cyber terms, but he just looked back at the smiling

Kim Son Tau who went on to explain,

"Dokkaebi are from Korean folklore, you would know them as goblins and these ones interact with humans."

"So, does Emerson have a download?"

"Yes, he has a copy including all the data."

"But he can't use it, you're telling us?"

"That is correct."

"Could he break or bypass to access the files?"

"There would be a small chance, but it would take him approximately thirty years based on my estimation of what I used as the key."

"And why couldn't he get the key?"

"Dragon Pearl by Yoon Ha Lee is a book I can recite from memory and the pages are the key, if you find the Dokkaebi in the files, and I worked a random, back-to-front, four plus four minus three, sequence."

At this point, apart from Kimmy, all the other men around the table were looking as if they were on a different planet talking to ET. It was Tim who brought everyone back to earth.

"So, the worst-case scenario is we have thirty years to find him and retrieve the files?"

"Yes, but remember it is a copy of the files, so if you have a good computer person, get them to do what I did, go back into the exchange, download all the information and replace it into new files. It would only give him access to useless expired files in maybe thirty years."

Bob stood and asked if anyone needed a refill, as he sure did, and went to the bar. He was joined by Jeff and George, and they looked around as Kimmy was explaining how he had installed his safety protocols and the process to salvage the securities market. As the fresh drinks appeared on the bar and Bob paid, George took a sip and said to Jeff,

"Be easier if you just employ Kimmy and let him clean the mess up and put it back together."

Jeff looked at George and you could see in his face all the lights came on and the fairground rides began spinning again, as he took his drink and hurriedly returned to the table, leaving George and Bob at the bar.

51

A week passed and as Bob walked into the Lord Nelson, immediately the barman saw him and took a couple of Guinness glasses from the shelf and began pouring. He smiled, put them on the bar and simply said, "Garden."

George put his hand up as Bob entered the garden area and as he wandered over, George stood and took one of the pints off him, placing it by the nearly empty glass on the table and sat down in time with Bob.

"First things first Bob, how's Sally?"

"She is fine now but gave me a good dressing down after I'd explained the events of the last few weeks. Apparently, she should have been here to support me."

George chuckled and raised his glass to salute either Bob's telling off or as recognition of the willpower of Sally Kennedy.

"The good news is that our friends in MI5 say that there can't be any link back to us, now that they have all the information and have taken control of everything."

It was Bob's turn to raise his glass and nod approval.

George emptied the last of his first pint and took a couple of sips of the fresh, cold Guinness Bob had brought out; putting the glass down, he adjusted slightly as if getting comfortable.

"Right, brace yourself, Bob, I have a few things to update you on that Tim has revealed to me in the last couple of days."

George started with how both Anderson and Daniels had broken their silence once they had realised Georgina Williams had done a runner. Both officers realised they had been hung out to dry and knew they were looking at some considerable jail time, so they'd decided that by fully cooperating they may possibly get sent down somewhere a little easier where they stood a chance of getting through unscathed.

"Their stories are still a bit thin in places, regarding the fatal fires and they're both sticking to their versions that from the fire service investigation at the time and the reports given, that the deaths were accidental, and they were not involved before the fires."

Bob shook his head. "Accidental my arse, any fire investigator would find flaws in that."

"Yes, but the problem is the bodies were very quickly disposed of which hangs with Williams, and the other paperwork was completed by senior fire officers, not them, although those reports have since been found in a lock-up linked to both of them."

Bob couldn't hide his frustration but accepted it, then added,

"I take it you know Area Manager Jeff Sykes has been taken into custody, along with SO Drayton?"

George nodded. "And again, I hear there's a blame game going on between the two of them. Drayton reckons Sykes ordered him to trial a quick-fire investigation and handover to police and Sykes denies that, saying he wanted him to do an efficiency investigation but without cutting corners."

Bob nearly choked on his beer, put his glass down looked across at George as if he had suddenly grown a pumpkin on his head and in the moment, George put his hand up before Bob could say anything.

"Don't worry, everything we had from our secret visit and your brief notes you'd put together from the first job, were in the hands of the interviewing officers who cut them into little pieces. You never know they may even share a cell with Daniels and Anderson."

That remark put a smile back on Bob's face and again he raised his glass.

"Get another couple of pints, Bob, and I will put another smile on your face thanks to MI5's and MI6's new cyber warrior."

Bob knew at once that he meant Kimmy and made the quick trip to the bar to freshen their glasses and returned sitting down like an expectant father, wanting to know is it a boy or a girl?

"Georgina Williams was obviously one of the bigger players in the whole set up but she also somehow managed to disappear without a trace," George paused to take another sip of his drink. "That was until Kimmy found her in the Caribbean on a small island posing as an author."

"How did he manage that?" Bob asked.

"I asked the same thing, but they wouldn't go into too much detail; although, they did point out that their newly-acquired asset is a master at aligning times from CCTV and security cameras and linking satellites."

Bob was never a techno sort of person; every year he still bought an A4 diary to write down his appointments, meetings and anything he needed to remember, so he asked George to explain it a bit more.

"The short version is he asked for a timeline from the moment she had gone off the grid, which they got from the last CCTV footage between Cable Street and Pinchin Lane. He started to check the movement of an Audi SUV which was picked up and found heading to Grays, then spotted in a rail station car park next to a van which was then traced heading into the docks. Finally, he managed to select a satellite over Tilbury Docks and logged the ships that left over the next twenty-four hours."

"That's a lot of shipping George."

"Yep, but most of it headed out across the Atlantic. So, after calculating speeds of vessels to designated ports and images without anything like a helicopter showing up, he found one ship the MV Doumo had slowed down just west of the Bahamas.

After finding a few more satellites, he picked up a small boat, probably a motor cruiser, and what appeared to be a ship-to-ship exchange with two people getting off the container ship and a large case going the other way, which I assume was a payment of some kind."

"How can he be sure that was Williams?"

"Don't ask me how but he tracked the boat around four hundred miles to a place called Matthew Town on the Inagua Islands, and they assumed they had disembarked at night because the boat was picked up heading back to the Bahamas the next day."

George went on to explain that the Matthew Town police station was contacted, requesting information on any new arrivals on the island which led to a copy of a driving license being emailed over of Miss Geena Wilson, living at a newly-rented home in the town.

"Clever to change the name but keep it similar to her own name, makes it easier when writing a signature," Bob said.

"MI6 didn't want to stir things up too much without drawing attention to the problems here at home, so they passed some information onto the American DEA who, along with local officials, carried out a raid yesterday and arrested her for being involved in drug trafficking. They've taken her to Puerto Rico for questioning."

"And what of Emerson?"

"Nothing so far, a private plane headed to Mexico and then onto South America, stopping at Ecuador, Bolivia and Brazil, before heading back to Florida and flying back to Madrid."

"He's just vanished then?"

"It seems that way at the moment, but he may surface soon because Kimmy has begun his work cleaning the securities market and when it becomes clear to Emerson he can't access the stuff, he's going to be mightily pissed."

They both raised their glasses at George's last comment and took a big gulp each.

52

The evening air was warm but not uncomfortable in the small Italian restaurant just across the road from the Alfredo Salazar Monument in Lima and the view out across the Pacific Ocean was epic. Emerson Jacobs and Danielle had chosen a table on a small, outside decked area but in the shade of a large parasol. Both had a glass of Pisco in front of them, the locals' favourite drink, which was like a grape brandy. Emerson's was a straight one, but Danielle had some soda water to ease down the kick a little. Both were dressed as tourists, but it seemed Emerson had gone for the classic fifties look with a pair of white chinos, white shirt and a white Panama hat, while Danielle was wearing black cargo shorts, a lemon-coloured blouse, flip flops and sunglasses. They were both looking at the menus and after a minute or two, Danielle looked up.

"Did you work out what happened to Danny?"

"Nothing definitive but it was definitely his body that was found in the unit after the fire."

"And the Korean?"

"He's disappeared without trace. I've found nothing through passport controls on any ports or flights, so I'm assuming he's gone to ground."

"Don't you think it's a bit odd though? Danny was a professional."

"There are a few scenarios I have played out in my head. Danny made a mistake with the timers, but Kimmy's body would have been found as well. Kimmy could have surprised him and managed to get out before the explosion, or the only other thing was there was an outside influence."

"Who could that be though? The links were set up to reduce

things finding their way back."

"Kyle Greenwood reported to you and Danny where is he now?"

"Greenwood was a weasel who knew his place, no he's not your man and anyway, he knew what would happen if we found out. But I will locate him soon enough and make sure he stays silent."

They returned to the menus and after another couple of minutes, had both decided on the lobster-stuffed ravioli in shrimp chupe sauce. They caught the attention of the waiter who came over to take their order, to which Emerson added a bottle of champagne. Returning to their conversation, it was Danielle who raised the issue of the download problems which she had been informed of when they first arrived in Peru.

"Why won't the files open for you?"

"I think Kimmy put some protection on it, the crafty little shit, but I know it can be broken, I'm just not sure how long it's going to take."

Danielle nodded and knew Emerson would find the means to resolve the problem eventually.

"Anyway, that is my problem to resolve and tomorrow, I want you to head up to the Chillon River in the Callao Region to look at another industrial unit that may be suitable for us to start up again."

"Yes, Sir, do you have any building plans or blueprints?"

"They can be picked up from the man that will be meeting you there in the morning, a Carlos Vargas."

The waiter served their meals and a few seconds later, returned with a champagne bucket and an open bottle of Intipalka Extra Brut which although Danielle chuckled at the name, Emerson took a sip and said, " It's actually not too bad."

They then proceeded to eat their meals and ordered some

Lacuma ice cream with peaches to finish. The waiter returned and enquired if they needed anything else or some coffee, but Emerson only asked for the bill.

The bill was paid in cash with a paltry tip, and they were out on the pavement and heading back to their hotel, which was somewhere Emerson wanted to be out of in the next day or two, and into a private villa on the La Punta Peninsula, which was all in hand. It took them about twenty minutes to walk to the hotel which overlooked the Parque Salazar and by the time they had arrived, they were both beginning to sweat profusely, something they put down to the 30-degree sunny day. But by the time they had exited the lift on the thirteenth floor, they began to feel a little nauseous. As they entered their adjoining rooms, they imagined it was due to overdoing the mix of rich food, alcohol and the dry warm climate. Emerson didn't speak as he entered, and he barely heard Danielle say, "See you in the morning."

As they shut their doors, they hadn't noticed the two men who had been standing in the fire exit stairwell and who as the doors closed looked at each other and nodded. One then looked at his watch while the other sent a text message on his mobile.

Emerson walked into the bathroom and splashed some cold water on his face and headed back to lie down on his bed. He sat on the bed, removed his shoes and as he was about to lie down, the hotel phone rang. Thinking it could be news about the villa, he answered it rather than getting his head down.

"Ciao, Mr Jacobs."

Emerson knew the accent was Italian but only a native of the country would have picked up, it was a Romanesco accent.

"Who is this?" he slurred a little, feeling like the Pisco was finally taking its toll.

"My name is Alessandro Lombardi, and I am the Deus Vindicta when people get caught with their hand in his Holiness's pocket."

Although Emerson's body was struggling, his brain was

suddenly on high alert.

Alessandro continued,

"Some days ago, you thought you could sneak into the Deus Aurum undetected, but you were sadly wrong and you misjudged our protection program. You see the Ezra Gateway is exactly that, there are no obstacles and like in faith, you must take the step through without hesitation. Your ghost step programme was picked up straight away which allowed us to track you back within hours without your knowledge."

Emerson's body was failing but his mind was clear, and he began to get a nasty feeling and as he attempted to try and bargain for his safety, or even his life, nothing came from his lips. He dropped the phone and fell from the bed onto the floor as Alessandro began what would be the last words spoken down the phone, not that Emerson would hear them.

"The thing is, Mr Jacobs, there is no excuse for stealing from God, there is only damnation and right now your body is shutting down which will then be followed by your brain in the next eight to ten minutes, or maybe a little longer. Of all the places to eat, you choose an Italian restaurant, so we arranged for a special chupe sauce with added Tetrodotoxin from the puffer fish which has been your downfall, may God have mercy on your soul."

The line went dead and ten minutes later, the two Italian men from outside in the stairwell entered both rooms to check for any vital signs on the bodies, then placed half-eaten Chinese takeaway pots of noodles by their beds and left the rooms as they found them. Each pot was heavily laced with Tetrodotoxin and marked up with a phoney street vendor name.

Acknowledgements

Thanks to my wife, Kate, for her support in the new direction I took when deciding to write this book. Also to Trish for her words of wisdom and feedback from first readings.

This book is especially for fire service men and women everywhere.

About Terry Hopkins

Born on the Isle of Wight in 1967 my father was a serving Fire Officer for the Isle of Wight Fire Brigade, as was my godfather Terry Jones who I was named after.

After leaving school and college I took a five-year spell in electrical and electronics engineering before following in my father's footsteps. A short stint in the retained service was followed by becoming a wholetime fireman as it still was then in January of '92.

Over the next thirty years of operational service from the operational shift system to operational support and planning on days and a short stint in charge of White Watch which was the best job ever with the best group of firefighters on the Island (in my opinion). The final next six years came about after a service switch around and I was moved into the Fire Safety Enforcement Team which became one of the most enjoyable times of my career.

From my first job as a 'probi' extinguishing a wooden pallet with Red Watch on Mill Street to being the lead Fire Safety Officer for the Isle of Wight and the last couple of years under Hampshire and The Isle of Wight Fire and Rescue Service still learning new things it has been quite a journey.

My time now is spent between writing, playing golf and spending time with family.

Available worldwide from Amazon

Michael Terence Publishing

www.mtp.agency

www.facebook.com/mtp.agency

@mtp_agency

Printed in Great Britain
by Amazon

23007692R00098